FINDING THE
BLUESTOCKING'S HEART

THE COLCHESTER SISTERS

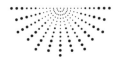

CHARLOTTE DARCY

FAIR HAVENS BOOKS

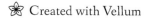

INTRODUCTION

Sweet Regency Romance

This is a complete story and can be read alone but it is the third of three books about the three Colchester sisters. If you missed the first book you can grab it here

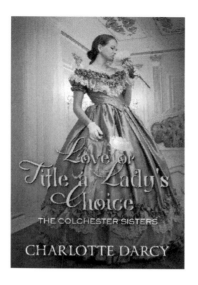

Or book 2 here

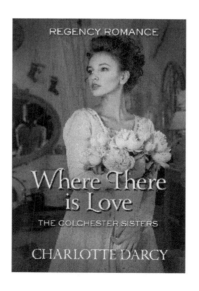

Charlotte Darcy writes sweet Regency romance that will take you back to a time when life was a little more magical.

Fall in love again,

Charlotte Darcy

CHAPTER ONE

"*V*erity, you are quiet," Amos said as he and his sister walked arm in arm through the grounds of their father's estate.

"I am quiet, I know. I am a little lost without Esme and Jane here," she smiled up sadly at him.

"I am a poor substitute for a sister, I daresay."

"Oh no, Amos. You are not a substitute at all. You are a brother, a very fine brother. I do not seek to fill that chasm with you. You occupy your own place in my world and it is an important one. I miss our sisters and I will just have to miss them. I cannot replace them with you any more than I could ever replace you with them." Verity was as earnest as always.

"My dear Verity, there is even a sense of logic and reason to your grief." Amos laughed.

"But I am not grieving, Amos, I am only sad. I still see Jane so often and Esme too, although I see much less of her. I have not lost them forever."

"You see things so clearly that I sometimes wonder if there is just a little too much clarity in your world." He patted her hand as it rested on his arm.

"How can a person see things too clearly?" She looked sideways at him quizzically.

"If I was as clever as you, I might be able to explain it. But since I am not, I think I should just keep quiet." He laughed, and she continued to look at him with confusion. "It is just a feeling I have. I suppose I would like to see a little happiness in your life."

"What does that have to do with seeing things clearly?"

"Oh, Verity! You are so serious. I think that is what I am trying to say. Even helping Jane to find her own true love, that wonderful romance, has not changed you." He was still laughing. "You are the same Verity as ever you were."

"Of course, I am. Why should I have changed?"

"I just thought you might have seen just what you were missing out on when you helped to bring Jane and Richard together. I hoped it might have given you some aspirations of your own. Perhaps not as romantic as Jane's aspirations always were, but romantic nonetheless."

"You think because I am not romantic like Jane that I am not happy? That does not make sense. People are all different and their happiness is specific to them."

"Of course, it is. Happiness is *specific!*" he said a little sarcastically.

"Well, it is!" Verity said, and began to grow exasperated with the conversation. "I know what it is you are trying to say to me, Amos, and I suppose I appear to you to be a little obtuse for not agreeing wholeheartedly. But you have to understand that when I say all people are different, I include myself. I am not looking for the fairy-tale marriage that was Esme's, nor am I looking for the great romance that Jane sought. I am not looking for any of these things, Amos, and I wish that you would simply understand that *that* is who I am."

"Oh, please do not be angry with me," Amos said, his face full of boyish apology. "Not when you are my favorite sister."

"Now you are just trying to flatter me to get yourself out of trouble," Verity said waspishly.

"I am, my dear. Is it working?" He grinned at her and Verity could not help but laugh.

And she knew that she really was Amos's favorite. Perhaps not favorite, but he certainly had a great fondness for the youngest of his siblings. There were almost ten years between them but unlike most brothers, Amos truly seemed to enjoy her company.

"Yes, it is working," Verity said truthfully. "What a good brother you are. I should not tell you off when you have been kind enough to spend your afternoon with me. Most brothers would be out hunting or working or doing any one of the hundred things that meant they did not have to pander to a lonely sister."

"I am not pandering to you, my dear. I have always enjoyed your company as well you know. You are just unusual enough to be interesting." He teased her.

"Well, that *is* kind of you." Verity decided on a little teasing of her. "I think most people find me just unusual enough to be avoidable."

"Perhaps if you had friends younger than Mrs. Barton. Really, she is older than Mama."

"What? What if I had friends younger than Mrs. Barton?" Verity said a little confused.

"Well, I just think that you would be out in the world more, Verity. The assembly rooms or attending the buffets and dances you ordinarily find some way to get out of. If you had younger friends, I think you would enjoy things more." Amos led her along a little path lined with yew trees to a beautiful and ornate wrought iron bench just beyond. "So, shall we sit for a while? I know it is a little chilly and we can return to the house if you would prefer."

"No, I do not want to go back to the house just yet, Amos," Verity said, thinking that it would be best for the two of them to talk thoroughly before they returned.

She could see that Amos still had all his old concerns for her and she needed to soothe his fears. If she did not, he would continue to interfere, and she was finding it a little draining.

"Are you angry with me again, Verity?" he asked as the two sat side-by-side and stared out over their father's grounds.

"No, I am not angry with you. And I do not want to upset you either, Amos, but I am bound to tell you that I would have friends closer to my own age if they were at all interested in me. But they are not, you see, and so I gravitate towards the people who are." She paused for a moment and tried to find the right tone.

She did not want to make Amos feel sad for her circumstances, neither did she want to make him feel responsible for her in any way. But if she did not explain things to him just as they were, he would continue trying to change her. And Verity Colchester did not want to be changed.

"I have always understood that to have an abundance of female friends of my own age that I must turn myself into something I am not. I would have to keep quiet about my interests, I would certainly never be able to bring up the subject of the microscope that

Papa recently bought me," she laughed and was pleased when Amos did the same. "I would have to deny my interest in architecture, botany, science of any kind, almost everything that I enjoy. In short, I would have to give up being myself, Amos."

"I would not like to see that," he said solemnly.

"No, neither would I. And it is for that very reason that I am not searching for the perfect union. In fact, perfect or not, I am not searching for a union of any kind. I am in a very fortunate position, am I not? To have parents who would not push me... and a brother who, when he inherits, will let me stay here forever. If that is still your intention." She gave him a rueful smile.

"Verity, I would be happy to keep you here with me forever, I really would. And I would do so for my own selfish reasons, for I could never imagine being pleased to part with you. But at the same time, I want more for you in this life than to watch everybody else's children being raised. I want you to have marriage and a home. You deserve it."

"But I do not want it, Amos. You must understand, you are wishing for me things that I would not wish for myself. I do not want to be denied my interests, I do not want my intelligence to be forced into a dark corner until it does not exist anymore."

"You look rather bleakly upon us men, sister. We are not all the same. I would never expect you to be anything other than yourself."

"But that is you, Amos. It does not describe the vast majority."

"You really are quite determined, are you not?"

"I am determined, Amos. I have my interests and I do not want to give them up. I do not want to wait until I am a widow like Aunt Mary before I am able to pick up the reins of my life again. Really, I had no idea what an interesting person she was until that dreadful husband of hers passed away. She could not be herself in safety whilst that man still walked the earth. Really, it is such an awful thing that I wonder you can even ask me to explain myself."

"But what if you met a man who was different? One who loved you for everything that you are and wanted you to remain yourself at all times? What would you do then?"

"I would write it down in one of Jane's romance novels, for such a man does not exist," Verity said with a laugh before getting hurriedly to her feet. "Come, let us go inside now. I really am a little cold."

As they walked arm in arm back towards the house, Verity sincerely hoped that she had laid Amos' fears to rest if only for a little while.

CHAPTER TWO

*I*rving Ayres walked into Clarendon's gentlemen's club with quiet, well-hidden amusement. He was ushered through the entrance hall to a small office where he was very quickly signed in as the guest of Amos Colchester.

Everywhere he went the walls were covered with dark wood paneling. The curtains and rugs were all in the deepest, plainest red, and there were portraits everywhere of notable former members; men for whom death was the only thing which could force them to relinquish their membership at Clarendon's.

As nicely as the place was kept, he could still detect the faint aroma of tobacco smoke and liquor. Everything was so masculine, from the decor to the smell of the place that it was almost feral. There was a darkness to it, as if they dared not throw the shutters wide in case they found a group of unwanted women peering in through the windows.

Irving stifled a chuckle; he was here to meet his old school friend and he knew he must behave himself. Although, why a man as bright and friendly as Amos would choose to spend so many of his evenings at Clarendon's was beyond him.

Amos was a man whose life was constant movement; was always outside doing something, and the austere, sober maleness of the place seemed so at odds with his character.

"Ah, marvelous." Amos greeted him in the dining room with customary enthusiasm, much to the annoyed stares of some of the other, older men who were silently enjoying their meals. "I have already ordered for the pair of us, I do hope you do not mind, Irving?"

"Not at all," Irving smiled and sat down at the little table opposite Amos. "So, how are you? Well I hope?"

"Very well indeed, Irving. And you look jolly well, Sir, I must say."

"Perhaps so, but I believe I am developing the little aches and pains of one who is approaching thirty."

"Yes, as we all," Amos chuckled and looked over at a smartly dressed young man, one of the servants at the club, and nodded at him in silent request for him to fill their sherry glasses. "I must admit, at nearly thirty myself, I am starting to wonder if I am no longer a young man anymore," Amos went on.

"And yet it does not seem such a long time since we were boys at Eton, does it?"

"No, it does not." Amos treated the young man who had filled their glasses to a broad smile. "Thank you."

"Do you ever think of settling down in life, Amos? Or is it a little too early for you?" Irving asked from motives of only the very vaguest interest.

The truth was, that seemed to be the direction in which the conversation was naturally heading, although Irving was really not interested in such discussions.

"I think the time is coming, my dear fellow. I have it

narrowed down currently to a choice between three young ladies."

"Why am I not surprised?" Irving said and laughed genuinely. "But if none of them stands head and shoulders above the rest in your affections, Amos, I do not think that you are particularly well suited to any of them."

"Actually, that is a very sensible slice of advice."

"I am happy to help," Irving said and began to forget the oppressive decor of the gentlemen's club as he settled into his enjoyment of Amos's company.

"What about you, Irving? Any young lady of note on your horizon?"

"No, there is none," Irving said.

"You seem a little downcast, Irving. But surely a fine man such as yourself does not want for the attention of the ladies," Amos said quizzically, "you have that fine estate and are impressive in sport, if I remember correctly."

"I do not lack for female attention in truth. What I lack is female attention I have any time for," Irving said.

"Nobody who catches your eye?"

"They catch the eye, Amos, but failed to catch the imagination," Irving said, feeling suddenly hungry and wishing that the food Amos had ordered would soon arrive, whatever it was.

"Out of interest, Irving, why is that?" Amos, ordinarily a light-hearted sort of man who rarely seemed to pay full attention to anything, looked suddenly serious and leaned his elbows on the table between them and observed Irving rather closely.

"I suppose the fact is that most young women seem the same to me. They are all looking for something that they have been forced to believe is absolutely essential to their very existence. And in many cases, it is."

"And that is?"

"A good marriage. A man who will be able to provide for them. And so that they do not have to live in reduced circumstances or fear of starving to death, most of them will do absolutely anything to achieve that stability. And who can blame them, Amos? When those are the options they are handed, who on earth can blame them?"

"Would it not then be a kindness to marry one of them, my dear chap?"

"Simplistically, yes." Irving shrugged. "But I am afraid that I do not want to be married to a woman who only wants to please out of a secret struggle to survive. They are instructed by mothers who felt that same struggle, you see, and so I find it does not matter whose company I am in, it always seems the same. They are accomplished in arts they think pleasing to us. Simple, frivolous things which would not threaten any of us."

"Perhaps you ought to meet my sister," Amos said and laughed heartily. "You would certainly find her one who bucked that trend."

"I am sure," Irving said politely, having no desire at all to meet Amos' sister.

Irving really did wish that they could change the subject altogether. He had long wondered what life would be like if he were a married man but knew that he could not live such a stilted existence. With his own parents as an example, he could see quite clearly how such things worked.

His father had chosen his mother because there was

nothing about her to challenge him. She determinedly swallowed down her own intelligence and talents so that his might look all the more impressive. But his father had grown bored with such a woman, little understanding that it was nothing more than his very own demands which made her of such little interest to him. He lived in a world he had created and yet he resented the woman who had, like so many others, been coerced into their own blankness. And, of course, Irving's father, like so many other men, did not even see their own part in it. It was an offense and a tragedy all at once, one which Irving Ayres did not intend to involve himself in.

"So, you would be looking for a learned sort of a woman?"

"They are all learned, Amos. They are taught all manner of things and undoubtedly pick up no end of wonderful ideas on their own through books. And then, in the interest of survival, they forget all of it. Or deny ever having known it, at any rate."

"And I suppose you still have the same run of interests that kept you a little apart from the rest of us at school?" Amos said in a light-heartedly blunt manner that Irving had always liked for the very fact that he knew it to be entirely self-conscious.

"I am good at sports, as you say, but I am not a hunting man nor a socializer particularly." Irving began. "I like books, I always have. I like learning, expanding. I attend lectures now and again, evenings of interest. So yes, I daresay I do have the same run of interests, only I have added to them over the years." Irving was his own man and had long since given up feeling the need to apologize for his own character.

"That is excellent, Irving. Absolutely excellent," Amos said and seemed so pleased to hear that not much had changed about Irving over the years that it was a little unsettling.

"All right, all right!" Irving said somewhat loudly, drawing scowls from the old duffers all around them. "What is this all about?"

"Can one not simply give a compliment without suspicion?" Amos said, his eyes wide and his face full of boyish mischief.

"No, one cannot," Irving said and laughed. "Oh, let me hear it, whatever it is."

"You have seen through me." Amos shrugged expansively. "Perhaps there is something I would discuss with you over dinner." He went on as their food was finally delivered to their table.

"Very well," Irving said as he picked up his knife and fork.

CHAPTER THREE

"*I* was so pleased that you got in touch with me, Mr. Ayres. It has been such a long time since you have come to one of my evenings and I am bound to say that you have been sorely missed," Mrs. Barton said as she ushered Irving into the drawing room.

"The last two years have been rather trying, Mrs. Barton, what with the passing of my father and my own responsibilities now that I have taken over his estate," Irving said by way of explanation. "But things have settled again, and I thought it was time for me to take up some of my old pursuits and friendships."

"Well, I am glad," she said and smiled at him with

such warmth that he was relieved; she did not bear any grudge for not having seen him for so long. "And how is your mother, my dear?"

"She is coming along slowly, Mrs. Barton," he smiled, choosing not to tell that good woman that he had every hope of his mother finally coming to terms with the idea of thriving after so many years of darkness under the rule of his pernicious father.

"That is very good news," she said enthusiastically. "Now, let me get you to settle down somewhere so that you might enjoy this evening's talk in comfort."

"Thank you kindly," he said, his eyes hurriedly scanning the room for any sign of Verity.

He had never met any member of Amos' family before; they had been close enough at school, but not so close that holidays were spent in one another's homes.

Amos' description of his sister had been fulsome; a little woman with shining dark hair, a pale face, and green eyes. And, more likely than not, sitting alone.

It was the last of the descriptive points which had finally led him in the right direction, for sitting on a small couch entirely alone was a small young woman with dark hair. Whether or not she had green eyes he would only find out by getting a little closer.

"Mrs. Barton, who is that young lady who sits alone?" he asked as innocently as he could manage.

"That is Miss Verity Colchester, Mr. Ayres. You will not have met her here before, for she has only been coming to evenings here this last year, perhaps just a little more."

"And she has no company this evening?"

"She very rarely does. I know her mother, you see, and so her family realize that she is quite safe here."

"Oh, of course, Mrs. Barton. I meant no offense at all." Irving bowed a little in apology. "I just meant that I would be pleased for an introduction if she, like me, is without company this evening."

"Yes, of course." Mrs. Barton brightened immediately. "Although, I must tell you that she is rather *subdued* with conversation at times, especially if there is something of interest in what the speaker of the evening has to say."

"Then we shall be easy companions, if she will have

me," Irving said, relieved that he had identified Verity so quickly, but wondering if he would come to regret listening to any part of Amos' little plan.

The truth was that Irving had never been particularly tolerant of matchmakers and it was only that Amos proved to be the first male to approach him with just that intent, that he found his curiosity piqued.

Had Amos been one of his mother's friends, a kindly lady who thought she knew what was best for him, he probably would have dismissed her little proposal out of hand.

As Irving and Mrs. Barton approached Verity, he made a little study of her. She was waiting patiently for the speaker of the evening to begin, so patiently that she was rather still. She did not seem at all self-conscious in being there alone and neither did she fiddle or fidget to occupy herself or look about the room shyly in the hopes of some company.

She simply sat there with the air of a person who was perfectly content to occupy their own space. She was neither ashamed nor proud of her solo status, just accepting of it. And whilst there did not seem to be anything particularly forceful about her, Irving could not help but already think her rather bold.

"Miss Colchester, would you allow me to introduce a dear friend of mine? One I have not seen for some time?" Mrs. Barton began brightly.

"Yes, of course," Verity said in a tone which could not be deciphered.

She looked up at Irving before slowly rising to her feet and smiling at him benignly. So benignly that he thought she likely understood the mechanism of introduction very well and could follow its little laws without being at all interested in it.

"This is Mr. Irving Ayres, Miss Colchester. I do believe he is greatly interested in botany as are you," Mrs. Barton said with a flourish as if he was an inattentive son whom she was desperately trying to find a wife for.

"I am very pleased to meet you, Mr. Ayres," Verity said and inclined her head in a manner that, if not entirely graceful, was very neat and efficient.

"And I am very pleased to meet you too, Miss

Colchester," he said and bowed. "I wonder if you would mind at all if I sat with you for a while?"

"No, not at all. There is plenty of space," she said and looked down at the couch and then back up at him. "By all means."

"Thank you," he said and waved a hand to indicate that she ought to sit first.

Mrs. Barton smiled at him as if she had accomplished some wonderful achievement. She went on to look about the room to be sure that her guests were all comfortable and well attended to.

"Now, if you will excuse me, I must see if Mr. Winstanley is ready to give his talk," Mrs. Barton began. "Oh, I do hope that everybody will find it interesting. I hope he will not spend too much time talking about microscopes," she said and sounded a little flustered before disappearing.

A maid approached with a tray of well filled sherry glasses and Irving smiled as he took two of them, handing one to Verity without a word.

"Thank you, Mr. Ayres," she said politely.

"Do you have a great interest in botany, Miss

Colchester?" he asked, wondering how to begin a conversation with her.

On closer inspection, Amos' youngest sister was really rather beautiful. She had the strangest expression, one which seemed to move between blank contentment and fierce inquisitiveness. She looked one moment at peace and as if there was not a single thought in her head, and the next, her green eyes were narrowed to slits looking about the room for any sign that the speaker was about to begin.

"Yes, it is a subject I enjoy very well."

"As do I And I am bound to disagree with Mrs. Barton in my quiet hope that Mr. Winstanley spends a good deal of the talk concentrating upon microscopes. I have lately purchased one for myself, you see."

"Have you?" Suddenly, Verity was animated. Her green eyes were no longer narrowed into slits but rather wide with interest. "I have a microscope myself, Sir. My father bought it for me last year and I do not think I have made the best use of it so far. I was hoping for some ideas this evening and, like you,

I am hoping that Mr. Winstanley talks greatly on the subject."

"Then here is hoping that we both get our wish," Irving said and raised his sherry glass in her direction.

He was surprised when she did the same. She was certainly not an effusively friendly young woman and he could hardly imagine her being one to trip over her own skirts to impress during an introduction. But it was clear that she liked the idea of him sharing her interest in a subject about which she seemed to be quite excited.

Already, Miss Verity Colchester was not at all as he had expected. In truth, he had never imagined that she would be anything like her brother's description. He had assumed that Amos had simply told him what he wanted to hear in the hopes of finding a suitor he could trust for his beloved sister.

But in her own way, Verity had already surpassed Amos' description. There was something about her that already had Irving's interest.

And interest, Irving knew, was a vital ingredient

which had been elusive thus far in his search for female company.

When Mr. Winstanley took his place at the far end of the room and set a large brass microscope on the long table which had been set up expressly for him, Irving thought that, all in all, he was about to have a very enjoyable evening indeed.

CHAPTER FOUR

or three days following her evening at Mrs. Barton's house, Verity had been getting the very most out of the microscope her father had bought for her. Mr. Winstanley, in his talk, had suggested all manner of things to study under magnification that she had not even thought of before and she was really very pleased that she had gone.

The only thing that she was missing was a small piece of tree bark and so she had to go a little further afield to find it, given that her father would not allow her to take her tiny pocketknife to any one of the trees on his estate.

She had been in the woodland for some time,

enjoying the absolute peace. And so, when that peace was finally shattered, Verity was taken aback.

"Miss Colchester?" She looked around sharply to see none other than Mr Ayres standing behind her. "Forgive me, I hope I did not startle you. It is a very pleasant day, is it not? Perfect for a walk."

"Oh, Mr Ayres," Verity said, wondering at his sudden appearance. "Do you often walk in these woods?"

"Yes, very often," he said, and Verity wondered why it was she had never seen him there before.

But of course, she only walked there herself once or twice a week and it was perfectly possible that they had both enjoyed that place for years without ever coming upon one another once.

It would never have occurred to Verity that a man of recent acquaintance would have liked her well enough to seek her out and so she simply accepted the coincidence as just that; a coincidence.

"I am just gathering some samples for my microscope," Verity said, feeling the need to explain the small but fully-opened pocketknife in her gloved hand. "Specifically, tree bark." She held the knife out.

"Yes, Mr. Winstanley did rather open the whole business up, did he not? I must admit that I am one of the people he described in his talk, one who has simply studied a few leaves. I had never thought to cut berries and squash them on a slide to have a closer look at them, that is for certain," he laughed.

"And have you done that now, Mr Ayres? Have you cut berries and studied them?" Verity had quite forgotten about the berries and determined that she would do the same.

"It is not the season for berries yet, Miss Colchester," he said with a smile and she lightly tapped her forehead.

"Of course, silly me. I think I am getting a little too overexcited by all the possibilities of the microscope," she laughed, feeling strangely foolish for her mistake.

Ordinarily, Verity did not find herself feeling foolish about anything and she wondered why it was she cared at all about making such a small error in front of her new acquaintance.

"Although, the strawberries will be here soon. But I must admit, if I began to cut them, I would undoubtedly eat them." He smiled at her and she thought him very pleasant to look at.

He was a tall man, not quite as tall as Amos, but perhaps a little better built. He had dark blonde hair which was rather thick and perhaps a little overgrown, but nice, nonetheless. He was not dressed as well as he had been in Mrs. Barton's drawing room, but then he was wearing the practical attire of a man who had decided to spend his morning walking. And Verity, who had done the same, found a certain amount of admiration for it.

He wore black breeches and well-worn knee boots, boots which looked as if they had seen a good deal of walking in their time. The greatcoat he wore over his olive-green waistcoat was in cream, and was also far from new.

And yet she did not get the impression that he lacked for money, although to Verity, that hardly mattered at all. He was just a man who dressed appropriately for the task at hand and, although it was just a simple thing, it pleased Verity and she liked him all the better for it.

"Yes, I am rather partial to berries of all kinds. But perhaps I will sacrifice a slice to one of my slides when the time comes."

"And what of this tree bark? Have you had any success in cutting it?" he asked, eyeing the knife.

"The knife is a little small, but it is very sharp," she said, turning to the tree she had been facing when he had first come upon her. "Perhaps I will try it," she said and immediately began to carve a small incision.

It was a little tougher than she had expected but with the application of some moderate force, the bark yielded a little. She slid the blade of the knife beneath the incision she had made and used it as a lever, pulling the handle towards her until a sizeable piece of bark, almost three inches in length, came away.

"Oh yes, that was very neatly done," he said with interest and moved to stand beside her. "You shall have plenty there to look at when you get home."

"Yes," she said, already losing her attention a little to the piece of bark in her hand.

Still, as inattentive to him as she had suddenly

become, Verity realized that he had said nothing when she had used the knife. He did not try to overtake things by suggesting that he ought to do it for her, nor did he make any mumblings about her being careful not to cut herself or make a mess of her gloves.

Another point in his favor, she thought.

"It seems we both gained a good deal from our visit to Mrs. Barton this week. I must admit, I had forgotten how very interesting her *evenings* are."

"Oh yes, she works very hard to find the best speakers, I find," Verity agreed, sliding the piece of bark into her pocket before closing the knife and stowing it away also.

"I do hope that our paths will cross again in her drawing room at some point."

"So do I, Mr. Ayres," she answered a little mechanically, although she thought that he was pleasant company and clearly a very clever man.

"Tell me, Miss Colchester, do you ever attend the dance at the assembly rooms in town? I ask only because I am lately back in society after a period of mourning and adjustment and am keen to take up some of my old pursuits."

"No, I am not particularly fond of such things," Verity said truthfully. "I used to attend when my sisters were both at home, but since they are now both married, I have not bothered. They used to rather force me, you see. There was always some intrigue or other, some little excitement they thought to have there, but it was never particularly my choice."

"Oh, I see. Yes, quite so," he said and looked curiously disappointed.

"I could stand to be there before because I enjoyed my sisters' company so well," Verity went on, feeling she needed to explain and yet not really understanding why. "But without them I cannot imagine being well enough distracted that I would enjoy it."

"No, indeed," he said and smiled with a little less ease than before. "Well, I am keeping you from your microscope, Miss Colchester." He brightened, but she thought it was rather forced.

"It was nice to see you again," she said, feeling at a loss.

"It was nice to see you too," he said and bowed. "I shall bid you a good day, Miss Colchester." And with that he smiled and continued on his way.

Verity found herself watching his departing back and wondering why it was she felt a little disappointed by his sudden determination to be away from her.

Undoubtedly, she had done or said something which made her a little unusual to him, something which had made him decide, like so many before him, that her company was perhaps not quite what he had hoped it would be.

But whereas ordinarily she would have shrugged off such an idea and thought herself better off alone, Verity felt a little sorry that he had gone. The truth was that she found him rather interesting and it had been so nice to be in conversation with somebody who seemed to share at least one of her interests.

It was a rarity outside of Mrs. Barton's drawing room or one of the lectures in the town hall. And even in both of those places, Verity did not seem able to draw people towards her for long enough to enjoy such conversations.

But she could only be herself and, if that was a little strange to Mr. Ayres, there was nothing that Verity could do about it. And in truth, there was nothing she *would* do about it.

As disappointed as she felt, Verity could only be true to herself.

CHAPTER FIVE

"How very nice to see you again, Mrs. Ayres," Amos said with the open friendliness which had served to make him one of the more popular men in the county. "And what a great shame for me that you are already otherwise engaged for the afternoon," he went on, much to Irving's mother's delight.

"What a kind young man you are," she said in her sweet and gentle voice. "But I had promised Lady Fulton that I would help her with the church flower arrangements. Her turn has come around very quickly and whilst she is willing, she is not terribly experienced."

"I am sure your help is greatly needed, Mother." Irving kissed her cheek to send her on her way.

His mother was a kind and warm woman, one who had raised him well, despite the criticisms of her husband.

"Your mother is a dear," Amos said genuinely, the moment the two men had been served tea and were alone in the drawing room of Forton House.

"And one who has forced herself into a mourning period stretching almost two years. Mourning for a man who would have barely afforded her a month of the same, had their situations been reversed."

"I suppose marriage is a complicated thing at times," Amos said, treading carefully for once.

"No, it is an uncomplicated thing which has been made complicated by silly social games and a deep-rooted fear of approval of all society being withdrawn," Irving said and laughed when he saw the look on his friend's face. "What?"

"You remind me of Verity, she says things like that." Amos began to laugh also. "She recently told me that happiness is *specific*." He continued to chuckle.

"Specific to what?"

"Specific to each person." Amos supplied the vital piece.

"Oh, I see. Well, yes, of course it is," Irving said, wondering why Amos could not understand something so simple.

"I suppose it is," Amos went on. "I daresay what tickles me is that you and Verity are the only people I know who would look at the thing in so clean cut a fashion."

"I presume it is Verity you have come here to discuss today, Amos." Irving, still smarting from his disappointment of just days before, wanted his friend to get the point.

"Yes, I was keen to discover how you got on when you bumped into her, as it were."

"I think it is safe to say that I will not seek her out in such a fashion again," Irving said. "A device like that can surely only be used once before it becomes suspicious."

"But she did not suspect that you were there by

design, did she?" Amos asked and looked a little fractious.

"No, she accepted my explanation of being a regular walker there as fact, which of course it is. But not the only fact, I daresay."

"You need not look so morose about it, my dear chap. On any other day, you might well have bumped into her quite by coincidence."

"Yes, but I did not, did I?"

"And is that the source of the reluctance I am sensing? The idea of a little subterfuge?"

"No, it is not the source of my reluctance at all. Although I am bound to say that, when I look back upon it, this whole thing is a little underhanded."

"Let us get to under-handedness and other such similar questionable behaviors later on. Let us instead get to the root of your reluctance, Irving."

"My reluctance is very simple, Amos. Your sister is not the slightest bit interested in me. That being the case, I am afraid to tell you that your little plan has come to naught. Not that I did not do my best, for I did. But as I said, your sister is not at all interested."

"What on earth makes you say that?" Amos seemed so surprised to hear it that Irving found himself equally surprised. "No, that cannot be right."

"It is as I say, Amos. Just because you would wish to see your sister with a suitor does not mean that she will immediately like the one of your choosing."

"And if she knew that you *were* of my choosing, Irving, I could quite understand it, for I know Verity to be as stubborn as a mule and if she thought I had any hand in it at all, she would either dig in her little hooves or kick me," he laughed. "But it is not that which surprises me. Really, when I thought of every one of my acquaintances, you were the one who came to mind, the *only* one who came to mind, as a potential suitor for my sister. I know her so well and I would flatter myself that I know you too. I am certain that you would be a very good match for one another."

"And yet she is not interested, Amos. And in the end, yours was hardly a scientific approach, was it?" He laughed, pouring tea for them both and enjoying the fact that his friend, always so bursting with confidence, had come hard up against a little failure for once. "You have not managed to pull our strings and twist the world to your liking, my dear friend," Irving laughed harder still, enjoying the look of disbelief on Amos' face more and more.

"I am not yet ready to concede," Amos said with some belligerence. "Tell me, why is it that you think my sister has no interest in you?"

"Because she made it very clear that she has no intention of attending the assembly rooms for the next dance. She had been perfectly agreeable up until that point, but firm in her refusal nonetheless."

"Did you find no common ground at all?"

"Yes, we did. As a matter of fact, when I first found her, she was collecting a sample of tree bark to inspect under her new microscope. We talked about it for some time, a continuance of all that we had learned at Mrs. Barton's little evening of interest."

"And you felt you were getting along well?" Amos was speaking slowly and thoughtfully, and Irving had a horrible feeling that this was not going to be the last of it.

"Yes, very well. Your sister was very animated in the discussion and I thought her very pleased with it."

"My dear fellow, my sister is, whilst adorable to me, a most unusual creature. She is likely unusual even by your standards, Irving. She is always very honest in her way. If she speaks to you with interest, it is because you are interesting her. If you fall upon a subject that she is not quite so enamored of, Verity cannot hide it. If you asked her something outright, there is something inside that woman which would force her to be absolutely honest."

"Which is commendable and, I am bound to say, even desirable to a man like me," Irving began. "But that being the case, I rather think that your sister made her feelings very clear in that rather honest way you have described."

"The only thing she made her feelings clear about, Irving, was attending dances at the assembly rooms." Amos began to laugh and seemed so relieved to have got to the bottom of it all that Irving was starting to wonder if the man had a point.

After all, who would know Verity better than her own brother?

"I will take your word for it," Irving said in what he hoped was a noncommittal tone.

"You could do more than take my word for it, my dear fellow. Listen, I will play upon her kindness and have her attend the assembly rooms with me on Friday. I am certain that you will soon discover that it is only the idea of such large public gatherings that my sister is not enamored of and that she did not mean to reject you. Knowing my sister as I do, she would never have realized that your inquiry was a little attempt at courtship. It would have sailed right past her consciousness, believe me. With Verity, one often has to make themselves very plain. With such things as the wants and feelings of others, she does not try to guess or pre-empt. She simply accepts everything at face value."

"All right, all right," Irving said and let out a great sigh. "I give in, Amos, but I will have you know that this is the *last time* that I will give in. If I perceive that your sister really does have no interest in me whatsoever, I will not continue to force the issue."

"That is the spirit, Irving!" Amos said and delightedly reached forward to help himself to some bread-and-butter from the tray.

CHAPTER SIX

"It is jolly charitable of you to come out with me this evening, sister," Amos said as the two of them walked arm in arm into the assembly rooms in town. "It is nice to get out every once in a while."

"Amos, you are rarely at home," Verity laughed. "I would imagine that it would be nice for you to stay in once in a while."

"I am a social creature, Verity, I cannot help it."

As always, Amos lifted her mood. He was wonderfully silly at times and never serious and Verity wondered if they got on so well as brother and sister because they were so very different. Perhaps it was simply because he so very obviously cared a great deal for her that she found it so easy to be in his company.

"And I am *not* a social creature, Amos."

"I know, and so my gratitude is tenfold for I know what it costs you to be here."

"It does not cost me to be here, Amos. I am just not fond of it as a way of spending my time. I would much rather choose an evening of interest over an evening of socializing, you see. And it is not the same since Esme and Jane went. At least then I could watch their antics and listen to their little dreams and help them." She shrugged. "That gave me some interest at least."

"Then perhaps you can help me," he said and scanned the room. "Perhaps I should have some little dreams that you can help me with."

"Amos, the only thing that you need help with is keeping women away, not attracting them to you. I rather think my talents as a matchmaker, however little they might be, are not required in this instance." Verity shook her head and laughed.

Her brother really was an attractive man in personality as well as looks and there was many a young woman in Colington who would very easily succumb to his charms.

"Amos! Amos Colchester!" A voice came from behind them and they turned as one to see who it was. "What a nice surprise to see you," the man went on and Verity's mouth fell open a little to realize that it was none other than Mr. Irving Ayres.

"As I live and breathe, if it is not Irving Ayres!" Amos said, giving every impression of knowing the man well. "Verity, please allow me to introduce you to a face from the past," he said, smiling broadly at her. "This is Mr. Irving Ayres. We were at Eton together."

"Oh, I see," Verity said, still reeling from the sudden appearance of the man she had tried not to think of since his hasty departure in the woods. "But we have already met, Amos."

"You have already met?" he said and seemed surprised as he turned to Mr. Ayres. "And where, pray, did you meet my sister?" He laughed.

"Your sister?" Mr. Ayres said with a look of

recognition. "Of course, I should have put the whole thing together at the time." He smiled directly at Verity. "We met in Mrs. Felicity Barton's drawing room but a fortnight ago."

"Oh dear, one of her evenings of interest?" Amos said and rolled his eyes.

"Well, it was of interest to me, Amos. Remembering you as I do, I daresay you would have fidgeted like a child and paid no attention whatsoever," Irving said, amusing Verity greatly.

"Forgive me, Mr. Ayres, perhaps I ought to have already known your name," Verity said, wondering if Amos had ever spoken of the man before.

"We were friends at school, Miss Colchester, but not so close as to particularly associate outside. But our paths cross from time to time and maturity has made us more tolerant of our differences than we used to be as boys."

"Goodness, yes, I can imagine that you were very different from one another," Verity said and looked doubtfully at Amos who she was certain would have sat inattentive and fidgeting in every lesson he took at Eton.

How well Mr. Ayres had described her brother, and how perceptive he must be.

"I say, Miss Meriton looks well this evening," Amos said, his attention being suddenly drawn to a lady who stood just a few feet away from them, a lady who was already enjoying his rather open stare.

"I do not think I am acquainted with her," Irving said and barely gave the pretty young woman a glance at all.

"I would beg you both to excuse me for just a few moments," Amos said, and Verity could see that he was entirely distracted. "I must just have a moment with that young lady and see if there is space on her dance card for me."

"By all means," Irving said.

"Yes, for I can see you will not be able to concentrate on anything else until you have done so," Verity laughed indulgently.

With nothing more than a quick smile, Amos walked the few short feet to Miss Meriton and immediately engaged her in lively conversation.

"I am afraid that my brother has a very short

attention span, especially when there is a beautiful lady in the room," Verity said by way of explanation.

"He was the same at school, in terms of short attention at any rate, for ladies were in short supply, pretty or otherwise. But I am bound to say that I always found your brother's company very pleasing. He is rather a happy soul, one who easily draws those around him."

"Yes, he is," Verity said, warming to him again and enjoying his praise of her beloved brother.

"I am surprised to see you here this evening, Miss Colchester. I mean, given your aversion to the assembly rooms."

"I am afraid that I was persuaded by my brother. He knows well how to play upon my sympathies, despite the fact that he does not truly need my sympathy in any way," Verity laughed. "And so here I am. And, as always, it is crowded and the only enjoyment I can find is watching other people and the silly way they seem to go about things."

"What do you mean?" Irving said and seemed suddenly interested, much to her surprise.

"Take my brother for example," Verity began. "He sees a young lady with whom he is already a little acquainted, one he already likes very much and is greatly attracted to. And in seeing her, he has decided to speak to her. And he does just that; he quite simply walks over to her and speaks," she said and could see that Irving was nodding in agreement. "But if you look across the room you will see a young man who is extraordinarily well-dressed." She lowered her voice so as not to be overheard, causing Irving to have to stand a little closer to her. "He is the one with a waistcoat that is so very golden in color and the painfully elaborate necktie." She raised her eyebrows and watched as Irving peered across the room.

"Oh yes, I see him," he said, lowering his voice also.

"Well, he has been staring over at a young lady just feet away from him for some time. She is the one with the dark curls and the blue gown." She looked into Irving's face for confirmation that he could see her. "They have looked at each other more than once in a way which suggests to me that they have already been introduced. And yet it seems that the young man will not stride up to her in the way that my brother might. Instead, he passes himself from conversation to conversation with this man and that man as he slowly creeps his way along the room. If I had money in my purse now, Sir, I would bet every penny of it that, if my rough calculations are correct, he will finally reach his quarry in about seven minutes from now." She looked back up at Mr. Ayres to find him smiling more broadly than she had yet seen him do.

"I can see the pattern already, Miss Colchester. He has moved on to his next conversation, see?" He pointed over with a nod of his head. "He is now speaking to the elderly gentleman with the old-fashioned and rather ill-fitting wig."

"There, you *do* see it," Verity said, pleased that Irving was content to join in with the only thing she found of interest to do in the assembly rooms.

"Indeed, I do see it. I suppose this is the sort of thing I have previously recognized but not really made much of. Look, there he goes again," Irving laughed. "He has already moved on from the elderly gentleman."

"He might even reach his quarry before my

estimation." Verity found herself smiling at Irving. "Do you have a pocket watch?"

"Indeed, I do," he said and pulled it from his waistcoat. "Another few minutes," he said immediately, perceiving that she meant to time the young man she was secretly studying.

"And all because he wants to dance with her. Really, would it not be simpler for him to do as Amos has just done and ask? Why is there always so much flutter and confusion when large groups of people are together? They seem to make things more complicated than they ought to be."

"There is much which is more complicated than it ought to be," he said and peered at his watch again. "Four minutes," he announced.

"I am afraid that this is how I spend my time when I come to the assembly rooms, Mr. Ayres," Verity said, wondering suddenly if he thought her a little odd.

"I think it is a most amusing use of time. If you do not enjoy being out in society like this, it is a very fine idea to have a secret pastime of your own."

"Although, I suppose it is not entirely a secret anymore."

"Have no fear, Miss Colchester, I will not say a word. I will not only keep your secret, but I will also take part in it. There, he has finally made his way to the young lady."

"How long?"

"With three minutes to spare," Irving laughed, and Verity thought him very pleasing. There was no hint that he was as uncomfortable with her as he had seemed to be the last time they spoke. "I think he has done more dancing to get to her than he will do when the two of them finally reach the dance floor."

"Yes indeed," Verity said and was so amused she laughed rather loudly. "A very good observation, Mr. Ayres."

"Thank you." He was equally amused. "Perhaps you would allow me to fetch you a glass of fruit punch? The table is a short distance and I believe that you are not a young woman who is terrified of her own company for three minutes."

"No, I am not," Verity said, feeling strangely drawn

by his most accurate observation. "But are you sure it will only be three minutes?" she said, realizing that she was, quite uncharacteristically, teasing him.

"I will leave this as surety that I shall return," he said and took her hand and turned it upward, dropping his pocket watch into her palm.

She watched him leave and smiled to herself. This time, he would be coming back, and Verity thought that she quite liked the idea of that.

CHAPTER SEVEN

The following day, Verity found that she felt a little listless. Her mother was out of the house and on some charitable mission or other, as was her wont for the last couple of years. And whilst Verity was pleased for her, she found she would have rather liked her company that afternoon.

Instead, with her father tucked away in his study working on the accounts, she found herself alone in the drawing room ideally pressing the keys on the piano.

She did not make any tune at all, just random notes to see if she could find one which resonated with her current mood.

The only problem was, Verity did not really know what her current mood was. She did not feel low spirited at all, but she was not entirely sure she was high-spirited either. She felt a little as if there was something she had forgotten, as if she had left home to go into town but had forgotten her purse. It was that sort of feeling, nothing catastrophic, just a needling sense that there was something she should be thinking about.

She was wondering idly if she were, perhaps, becoming unwell, when she thought of Mr. Irving Ayres quite out of the blue.

Verity really had enjoyed his company the previous evening and had been glad, in the end, that she had agreed to attend the assembly rooms with her brother after all. Even when she compared it to evenings spent there with her beloved sisters, Verity had had an uncommonly good time.

Irving Ayres had proved to be a most amusing man. But not amusing in the way that men often thought they were; no, he was truly amusing.

He made intelligent observations and voiced them well, making Verity laugh so much on one occasion that her brother had turned from his lively conversation with Miss Meriton to satisfy his curiosity for a moment.

But Amos had very much left her to it, hardly spending a moment with her for the rest of the evening. So, she thought that she could easily conclude that Irving Ayres was a good man, otherwise, Amos would not have left her alone with him. Not alone with him exactly, for Amos was only a few feet away. A casual observer would have thought everything entirely proper, that they were almost a part of the same party, so to speak.

But to all intents and purposes, Verity had enjoyed the entire evening in the sole company of Irving. And what was more, she had liked it.

Irving had looked very well indeed, a far cry from his well-worn walking apparel, that was for certain. He wore black trousers and tailcoat with a pale green waistcoat beneath. The contrast was subtle and striking all at once and the predominantly dark outfit suited his blonde hair and tanned skin very nicely.

When she thought about it, Verity realized that Irving was a very handsome man. No doubt his handsomeness would have been the very first thing her sister Jane would have fixed upon. But Verity had barely noticed it until he had become a little more interesting to her.

He was engaging conversation all round; he talked well of scientific subjects such as their shared interest of microscopes and was an amusing social commentator to boot.

Verity knew that she herself was a little cynical of society and its myriad motives, she had even been teased for it by almost every member of her family, but she had never felt able to give voice to her opinions of society to anybody else. And yet it was all very easy with Irving, for it was clear that he saw what she saw and perceived it in much the same way.

Verity was shaken from her reverie when her brother seemed to burst into the drawing room without any warning.

"Amos!" she said, drawing away from the piano.

"Forgive me, I could hear your beautiful playing from the hallway and thought I must come in and get the full benefit," he grinned at her.

"I was not playing, I was simply striking the occasional key."

"Yes, I perceived as much," he chuckled, "so, I actually thought I would come in here and find out why."

"Does there need to be a reason?"

"Oh, Verity, would you mind awfully unraveling just enough to talk to me properly?"

"All right, consider me unraveled, Amos," she said and wandered over to the fireplace. "Since it is only the two of us, shall we have tea a little early?"

"Not only have I already asked for tea to be sent, my dear, but I have put in a request that we each have a slice of that lemon cake cook made, the one with the sugary coating." He advanced into the room and sat down on the couch, patting the seat beside him to indicate that he would like her to join him.

"You are very attentive today."

"I am just hungry, and I have not been able to get the lemon cake out of my mind since my first slice yesterday."

"Well, I suppose at least you are honest." Verity sat down next to him and laid her hand in his. "So, what are you doing with yourself today?"

"Idling, much as normal," he said with a grin. "I have been in a little world of my own today, if I am honest. Miss Meriton is such a beauty, is she not?"

"She is very beautiful to look at, Amos," Verity said. "But what is she like? You seemed to talk to her for the entire evening."

"She certainly seemed like a very nice young lady."

"In other words, you were doing more staring than listening," Verity said with a mock exasperated sigh. "Really, Amos, you are nearly thirty. Is it not time that you learned to look beyond a pretty face?"

"And is it not time that *you* chose to *look* upon a pretty face once in a while?"

"What on earth do you mean?"

"Well, not a pretty face, but perhaps a handsome one." He shrugged and squirmed. "Not that I find Irving Ayres particularly handsome, but I believe young ladies find him so."

"Yes, he is a handsome man," Verity said and felt a little heat rising in her cheeks.

Ordinarily, Verity could have declared anybody to be handsome and been entirely unaffected by it. The truth of the matter was, she liked Irving. He seemed to have come out of the blue and landed in her world in a most pleasing way. But she had no idea how to say any of that to her brother without him teasing her terribly.

"But?" Amos said and rolled his eyes.

"But what?"

"Presumably there is something wrong with him."

"Such as what?" Verity said, feeling confused.

"Oh, so you find him handsome *and* agreeable? Well, that is a good start."

"A good start to what?"

"Really, you would try the patience of a most experienced interrogator. Why can you never elaborate?"

"I already have. You asked me if I think Irving handsome and agreeable and I said yes."

"No, you said nothing."

"Amos, you are wearing me out already," she said and took a deep breath. "Your friend, Mr. Ayres, is very pleasant. He is handsome and agreeable. There, are you satisfied?"

"Forgive me, I am interfering," he said with mock humility. "But I thought you might at least have invited the poor man for afternoon tea next week. After all, he is a new acquaintance of yours and you seemed to find things in common."

"Perhaps I *should* have invited him to tea," Verity said, almost to herself. "But I am afraid things like that do not occur to me by instinct. I know they ought to, Amos, but it seems that I am not built in that fashion."

"Well, there is no reason why you cannot still make an invitation, is there? I could give you his address and you could write to him."

"Oh, no," Verity said and felt suddenly a little panic stricken. "No, I do not think I would be at all comfortable with that."

"I wonder if you would be comfortable with *my*

inviting him? He is an old school friend, after all, and it would seem quite natural for me to invite him here, would it not? To have afternoon tea with us, of course, not just myself."

Verity gave it some thought. Perhaps that was the thing which had been niggling her, giving her the idea that there was something she had forgotten. And she really would like to see him again, for she could hardly say how much she had enjoyed herself at the assembly rooms.

"Very well, if you would like to invite your friend to afternoon tea, I have no objection to being here."

"If I did not know you as well as I do, I would find your response somewhat negative. But since I have great experience of your flat expressions, I shall take it that you would be pleased for me to invite him."

"You may take it as you wish, Amos."

"Then I shall do just that and say no more upon the subject. I can tell that I am on the verge of vexing you and I am not sure that it is a sensible course of action for me to take."

"No, it is not," Verity said sternly but laughed,

nonetheless. "Ah, here is tea. You have been saved by the arrival of lemon cake."

"Yet more reasons to like it," Amos said and squeezed her hand as the maid came into the room and set their tray down.

CHAPTER EIGHT

hilst Irving had been pleased to receive the invitation from Amos, he wondered if it had anything to do with Verity at all. A part of him had wanted to make some excuse, believing that this was simply nothing more than Amos' determination to have his sister and friend somehow joined.

But he had so enjoyed his evening spent in Verity's company at the assembly rooms that he knew he could not turn it down if there was any possibility at all that Verity would welcome his presence in her home.

It was a bright day and spring was most definitely edging ever closer towards summer, raising Irving's spirits as he made his way to the Colchester family estate.

He had never visited the home of his friend before and was pleased to find that it was very similar to his own in terms of wealth and station. He knew it ought not to matter, and yet he found the idea that they were of identical backgrounds rather comforting.

"Do come in, Irving." Amos greeted him warmly when he was shown into the drawing room.

"Good afternoon, Amos. I trust you are well?" he said, and Amos nodded vigorously in confirmation. "And Miss Colchester, how nice it is to see you again," he said, turning to her and bowing.

"Good afternoon, Mr. Ayres," she said and gave him that curious, perfunctory nod that he had seen before. "It is a very fine day, is it not?" she said hurriedly, as if trying hard to make the sort of conversation that one ordinarily would make with a new guest for afternoon tea.

"Very fine indeed," Irving said and wanted to stamp on his own foot tor not coming up with something better than a simple agreement.

"Well, take a seat. I am pleased to say that we will be able to offer you some very fine lemon cake this afternoon," Amos said with a flourish. "The cook made it for us last week for the first time and I was so pleased with it I begged her to make another one for today."

"Then I am looking forward to my tea better and better."

They all took their seats, Irving in an armchair and Amos and Verity side-by-side on the couch opposite. The room was very pleasant indeed, of a similar size to his own drawing room and decorated well, if not in the most up-to-the-minute style.

He allowed his eyes to flicker to Verity now and again, immediately taking in how beautiful she looked. She was wearing a light blue gown with short sleeves which had a pretty little frill of white lace around a modest neckline.

Her dark hair was coiled neatly at the back of her head, but it had been done so loosely, giving it a softness and a fullness that he thought suited her very well. And, as always, her intelligent green eyes against her pale skin were the highlight of her beauty.

"I am surprised not to see Miss Meriton here, Amos," Irving said, teasing his friend as a means of turning the conversation from the weather. "You seemed very well pleased with that young lady at the assembly rooms."

"I *was* very well pleased with her, it is true," Amos said and then paused for a rather lengthy period. "But I am not entirely sure I would invite her to afternoon tea."

"For heaven's sake, why not?" Verity asked and looked exasperated with her brother. "You spent the entire evening with her and ignored Irving and me entirely. Surely you did not desert us in such a fashion for a young lady you could take or leave."

"I am afraid that it is only in the days which have followed that I have decided that I could take or leave her." Amos shrugged.

"You are as fidgety and inattentive as ever, Amos," Irving said with a laugh. "But I daresay it is part of your charm."

"Oh, I rely upon it," Amos said and looked up as the maid came in bearing a well laden tea tray. "Ah, thank you, Muriel. Not a moment too soon for I am extraordinarily hungry."

The maid said nothing, she simply smiled in a way which suggested that Amos was always extraordinarily hungry.

"And how have you been, Miss Colchester?" Irving asked, feeling curiously nervous but knowing that he must draw her in somehow.

He could not spend the entire afternoon using Amos as a crutch to lean upon. He wanted to discover if he was simply there by Amos' design or if Verity truly wanted his company. And it seemed more important to him now than ever.

He had come to realize that what had begun as an act to simply appease an old friend, had now become something else. He had truly thought that he would meet once with Amos' sister, fulfill his little responsibility, and be done with it.

What he had not expected however, was to find himself thinking about that young woman more and more, remembering their conversations in such detail as he thought he might never forget them.

"I have been well, Mr. Ayres," she began little falteringly. "I cannot say that I have been greatly occupied, not with any physical activity. But I have been reading a good deal," she said, giving a very neat account of her diversions since he had last seen her.

"And what have you been reading, Miss Colchester?" he asked, hoping for that common ground which seemed to bind them a little.

Perhaps a little botany book or some technical pamphlet on microscopes? That would do very well to keep them talking, at any rate.

"I have been reading a book about Mr. Inigo Jones," she said with some caution, undoubtedly as a result of having those around her roll their eyes at such a pastime.

"Oh, the architect? Yes, I daresay that is very interesting," he said, inwardly rejoicing that she had struck upon yet another area of interest for him. "I am quite an admirer of that Roman type of architecture he blessed our country with."

"And so am I, Mr. Ayres. I think the buildings of the last century have such wonderful lines and gravitas. And I do believe that many of the buildings, if not all, owed much to Inigo Jones' vision... and please call me Verity."

He nodded and smiled. "Then you must call me Irving... I think our dear Inigo inspired a great many architects who followed him. And who would not be inspired by the Queen's House in Greenwich."

"Precisely," Verity said, sitting forward a little with those green eyes wide and engaged.

"Have you seen the Queen's House, Verity?"

"I have seen it twice, Irving. My father took me on both occasions because Amos would not." She gave an amusing sideways glance at her brother. "But I am bound to say that Amos missed out on a great treat."

"Yes, indeed. The Tulip Staircase alone is enough to render one speechless."

"I agree, Irving. I spent so long staring at it that I believe I remember every detail."

"The *Tulip Staircase?*" Amos said and winced and shrugged all at once.

"Oh, Amos, it is a beautiful spiral staircase in the Queen's House in Greenwich. It is absolutely glorious to stand beneath it and look up. It is such a large staircase and seems to spiral away into the heavens," Verity said wistfully.

Irving could not take his eyes from her; she was staring into the middle distance as if seeing the staircase again for the first time and she looked more beautiful than ever.

She was not a young woman who saw beauty only in her reflection or the cut of a gown, she saw it in stone structures and the magnified study of plant life. Verity Colchester was a woman with interests, and they were interests which clearly meant a great deal to her.

And in that much, Irving knew them to be the same.

"That is a perfect description, Verity," Irving said and knew that he was going to have a very fine afternoon indeed.

"Would you like some cake, Irving?" Verity asked brightly, leaning forward to the low table where the tray had been set.

"Yes, please," he said and smiled at her, pleased that she smiled back with equal warmth.

As the afternoon went on, Irving became more and more convinced that Verity had been very pleased for her brother to invite him for afternoon tea. As much as this was Amos' wish, it seemed to be Verity's also.

But he knew he could take nothing for granted, for she was most certainly not anything like any other young woman he had ever met.

Nonetheless, he allowed himself a little warm glimmer of hope that he might have finally found the woman he had searched for all these years.

CHAPTER NINE

*B*efore Irving had even left the drawing room on the afternoon he had come for tea, Verity had already decided to invite him to join her at a public lecture at the town hall.

Having discovered that he also enjoyed architecture, she had thought that he would make very fine company at such an event. Ordinarily, she would have begged Amos or one of her parents to go with her, but if Irving would agree to it, surely *he* could accompany her instead?

"Amos, could I please have Irving's address?" she said as the two of them ate a late breakfast together some days later.

"Yes, of course," Amos said and seemed strangely delighted. "Are you thinking to invite him to afternoon tea again? Or perhaps even dinner? I am sure that our parents would find him very fine company."

"No, I was not thinking of anything of that nature," Verity said airily, and Amos looked a little disappointed. "No, there is a lecture that I intend to go to at the end of the week. It is one of the town hall public lectures in that room they set aside for such things," she said and laughed when Amos pulled a face. He had attended with her on a number of occasions and it had been a most difficult thing to keep him still throughout. "It is about 18th-century architecture. That is why I was reading the book about Inigo Jones, you see. I have planned to attend this lecture and realize now that Irving might enjoy it also."

"And so, you were going to write to him to let him know that there is a lecture in the town hall?" Amos said and speared a cooked tomato, spraying the tablecloth with juice and pips. "Goodness, tomatoes are such awkward little devils."

"I have seen before how you struggle with them, my dear," Verity said in a quietly teasing tone.

"Really, I think it would be better if the cook mashed them. That way I would be safe."

"I do not think that the cook would mash tomatoes, Amos, even if you insisted. She has certain standards beneath which she would not dip, and I do believe that mashing tomatoes just because there is one man in the house who cannot quite manage them with grace would certainly qualify."

"I suppose that is a fair comment," he said and treated her to his customary boyish grin. "But we are getting off the subject. You intend to write to Irving and let him know that there is a lecture to be held in the town hall?"

"Yes, that is exactly what I intend to do. Although, I was going to suggest meeting him in the foyer so that we might sit together," Verity said simply.

"Without a chaperone of any kind?" Amos said cautiously.

"Why on earth would I need a chaperone to go to a lecture in the town hall? I know you have come with me in the past, but you do not enjoy it at all and if I am to have company there, I would not need you to concern yourself."

"No, that is not quite what I mean."

"Then would you explain yourself, brother, and I beg you to be plain," Verity said, wondering what his objections could possibly be.

"Well, I think it is customary for a young woman, when out with a man, to have some intermediary there." He shook his head in disbelief. "Really, so much of what is *normal* simply passes you by, does it not?"

"No, it does not. I fully understand the entire business of chaperones and young ladies not being trusted. Or perhaps it is men who are not trusted, I cannot say. My point is that it does not fit the circumstances."

"Are you quite sure it does not fit the circumstances?"

"I am certainly sure, but *you* do not seem to be. Perhaps, if you have some objections, you would be better to tell me about them."

"I do not object at all. Irving is a very fine man and I would trust him to look after you very well. And so, these are not objections, my dear, I suppose it is an observation."

"I really do not understand."

"Well, it rather strikes me that you and Irving are not simple acquaintances. You are not friends in the common way."

"Why not?" Verity said, a little defensively. "I like Irving and I am certain that he likes me. Why can we not be friends?"

"Verity, Verity, Verity," Amos laughed and shook his head, putting his knife and fork down on his plate. "I am trying to suggest that you might consider yourself and Irving to be a little more than friends. A little *better* than friends. Oh goodness, I shudder to use this word in your presence, but it is the only one which springs to mind."

"What word?"

"Romance," he said and winced so thoroughly that his eyes closed completely.

His wince continued, his mouth seemingly pulled up

in a garish sort of grin as if bracing himself against some physical assault he soon expected.

"Nothing romantic has passed between us at all, Amos. He is simply a very pleasant man who has the same interests that I enjoy. And I liked his conversation very well at afternoon tea. But that is not romance, brother."

"Very well, I will give you his address," Amos said, giving in and laughing for reasons she did not understand. "I do wish you would read between the lines sometimes though, Verity. Must you always stick absolutely to everything that is in black and white?"

"Everything that is in black-and-white is assured, Amos. Anything that is in between the lines, as you put it, is generally conjecture at best and fantasy at worst. I would much rather deal with what exists than what does not."

"I absolutely give in," Amos said. "I will write down Irving's address as soon as I am finished with breakfast and simply let you get on with it."

"Thank you," Verity said simply and reached for her tea.

"Except I would ask you to do one thing for me." Amos set off again, this time in a wheedling tone.

"And that is?"

"When you are sitting in this lecture at Irving's side, would you give some consideration to the exact nature of your acquaintanceship? I mean *really* consider it."

"Yes, of course," Verity said and was careful not to shrug.

In her heart, she knew what Amos was getting at for she was no fool. But she was not entirely sure about the whole business of romance, not even enough to say that she had any romantic feelings about Irving whatsoever.

"My dear Verity. You do exasperate me. But you amuse me in equal measure, so I could forgive you anything," Amos said and set about his breakfast once more.

"If that is supposed to be a compliment, brother, I daresay I have no choice but to accept it," Verity said and smiled at him, already looking forward to the prospect of seeing Irving again.

CHAPTER TEN

"I have never heard of this Irving of yours, Verity," Jane said in a breathless and excited whisper the moment her maid had left the sisters alone.

Within just five minutes, Verity was already regretting her decision to come to her sister for assistance in clarifying the whole business of romance. She had needed to find some answers and had thought Jane, newly married and still romantic despite her new status, would be the most sensible choice of confidante.

"Firstly, Jane, he is not *my* Irving," Verity said for the purpose of clarification. "And secondly, he was a friend of Amos at Eton. I gather he was not close enough a friend to join the hordes of fellows who used to descend upon our house in the summers," Verity laughed.

"Goodness, yes! Dear Amos, he was such a popular boy. I was always so excited when he brought a new friend home. They were invariably as silly as Amos and such wonderful fun."

"Well, Irving is not at all silly. I suppose that was why Amos never invited him to our home when he was younger. Although, he must be growing up a little, for he seems to like Irving very well now. Perhaps he has a better understanding of him now he has matured. Or at least matured as much as Amos is ever going to." Verity shrugged. "I daresay we never heard of Irving because he was not a *particular* school friend of Amos'."

"And he lives in the county?"

"Yes, he is much further west. We have very few acquaintances in common; there is just Mrs. Barton as far as I am aware. And he is not entirely a stranger to the assembly rooms, although I understand he has not attended much in the last two years since his father passed away. His mother is still growing used to a life without him."

"Oh, that is sad. They must have been very much in love." Jane was instantly glassy-eyed.

"From what Amos tells me, I should say not. The late Mr. Ayres was a controlling man who allowed his wife none of her own spirit for their entire marriage."

"Oh, I see." Jane's romantic notion was thwarted, and Verity felt sorry for it. "Then she must be relieved he is gone."

"I think it takes a prisoner some little while to get used to the idea of their freedom. Rather like Aunt Mary."

"But just think, when Aunt Mary finally realized her freedom, there was nothing to hold her back. Goodness, whoever would have known *she* was a woman of such a sharp tongue and sturdy opinions!" Jane winced.

"I like Aunt Mary," Verity said in simple defense of the woman. "I am glad I came here. To say it all out loud reminds me well why I have chosen a solitary path." She changed the subject abruptly.

"Oh, Verity, no!" Jane complained. "Just when I thought you were getting somewhere."

"Why must success for a woman be linked to marriage?" Verity said, realizing once again how very different they were as sisters.

"I am not thinking about success, Verity, I am thinking about happiness."

"I daresay I am too. I mean, Mrs. Ayres must have been unhappy. A clever woman so ignored and denied. She gave up her chance of happiness when she married."

"But it does not go without saying that marriage *leads* to unhappiness. What if that is where your happiness is, Verity? What if this Mr. Irving Ayres is the man you were meant to be with?"

"And what if his mother thought the same about his father?"

"Verity, you do not account for the fact that people often know exactly what it is they are getting into," Jane said in a surprisingly level and sensible tone. "We both know well that people marry for all sorts of reasons and love is only one of them. For most people, they marry for something that they need, do they not? A home, status, security. And I believe it is likely very true that people have a good idea of their marriage partner before they ever take their vows. It strikes me that you are afraid that you might not know a man's true character until you are married to him."

"I think it an eminently sensible fear," Verity said.

"Yes, because you think sensibly?"

"Yes."

"Rationally?"

"Yes."

"Because you are a very intelligent woman."

"Thank you," Verity said, unsure what was coming next.

"Then I am certain that you would know. You would easily work out a man's character before you agreed to the marriage. And it is yours to agree or deny, given the fortunate position you enjoy. The same position Esme and I enjoyed; that our family has no motives for us. We are already free, Verity."

"Oh," Verity said and sat up straighter on her chair in surprise.

"What is it?"

"That is the most sensible thing I have ever heard you say, Jane. And you reached the conclusion long before me. In fact, I did not reach it at all, not until you said it." Verity was wide-eyed.

"Well, you need not look so surprised!" Jane said and feigned offense. "I am sensible enough when I have a mind to be."

"Yes, you are!"

"I suppose it is a lifetime spent with you and your plain way of looking at things. I daresay some of it has rubbed off on me. One can only hope some of my tendency towards love and romance has rubbed off on you." Jane studied Verity doubtfully.

"You do not think so?" Verity said and wondered if there could be romance in her life; romance with Irving Ayres.

"Perhaps." Jane continued to study her. "Really, it is hard to tell with you; you so rarely show your feelings."

"Then I am no closer to understanding it all. I had hoped you would help me see it a little more clearly."

"Ah! I have it," Jane said and was excited once more. "A little test!"

"What test?"

"Think about your Irving. Really think about him. Look, close your eyes, Verity. You must enter into the spirit of it."

"Very well." Verity screwed her eyes up tight and Jane stifled a laugh.

"Good," she said and cleared her throat. "Now, imagine Irving. Picture him."

"Yes." Verity pictured him easily.

"Is he a handsome man?" Jane whispered.

"Yes, he is a very handsome man."

"Then imagine your favorite moment with him. A time when you felt yourself to be enjoying his company so well that nothing else mattered."

"I'll try," Verity said and was silent for some time.

"Do you have anything?" Jane whispered finally.

"Yes. We were at the assembly rooms watching a young man make such a ham-fisted performance of working his way across the room to speak to the young woman he liked. Irving was so amusing, and we talked all evening so comfortably."

"So, he was handsome and amusing? Fine company?"

"Yes," Verity said and felt her heart beginning to open.

"Now, imagine another scene altogether," Jane said, still speaking softly and making Verity feel as if she were in a relaxing, wonderful trance. "Irving is climbing up into a carriage. He lowers the window and looks out at you, his face so handsome. And then, as the carriage slowly draws away, he waves at you. He is going to live far, far away. And you wave back, knowing that you will never, ever see him again," Jane finished, and Verity's eyes flew open.

Her hand went instinctively to her chest, as if to soothe her heart. She glared at Jane, so aggrieved that she had turned a wonderful mental image into something so distressing.

"Jane! What did you do that for? That was unkind of you!" Verity accused.

"Then you are upset?"

"Yes, of course I am upset."

"Because you imagined how you would feel if you lost Irving for good?"

"Well..... yes."

"Then I do believe you are well on your way to falling in love, Verity," Jane said triumphantly. "You have passed the test. There is room in your heart for someone after all."

"Oh! Jane!" Verity said, feeling a little overwhelmed.

"Perhaps some more tea to settle you?" Jane smiled warmly as Verity scowled at her.

"Yes, I think so."

And, as they sat in silence for a while, Verity wondered if she really was falling in love after all.

CHAPTER ELEVEN

"*I* was very glad you wrote to me, Verity," Irving said the moment he arrived outside the town hall.

She saw him from the carriage and called out to him. Irving immediately helped her down, calling up to the driver that he need not worry to climb down.

"I am glad you could come. I should have mentioned the lecture when you came to us for afternoon tea, for I knew of it then," she laughed. "That was why I was reading about Inigo Jones in the first place. I was looking forward to the lecture and wanted to immerse myself in it all. When I saw your interest, I realized you would like such an evening. But it did not occur to me at the time to mention it. It is often the way, I am afraid."

"Because you were so caught up in your interest. There is nothing wrong with being passionate about such things. I am just glad it came to you in time for you to invite me," he smiled at her and Verity had a sense of ease; a sudden realization that he somehow understood how things were in Verity's day to day thinking.

"My family despairs of me at times. My lack of attention to certain details and my preoccupation with things they are not sure really matter," Verity admitted and was treated to a wonderful smile.

He really was handsome; even Jane would think so.

He was wearing black again, with a cream waistcoat and a necktie which reached high under his chin. Irving was indeed a well-dressed man.

"I think interests do matter; learning matters. We do not know all there is to know by the end of our tutoring, after all."

"No, Irving, I agree. I believe that the end of our tutoring is just the beginning. The only thing we have finished is learning what others would have us know. But they give us the tools to keep searching and learning."

"And it is lifelong," he smiled and held out his arm for her to take.

As they walked into the town hall arm in arm, Verity realized just why Amos had thought a chaperone might be in order. Irving did not feel like a simple friend, not now that she was actually touching him, albeit an innocent touch.

But he felt so fine, so tall and strong, and Verity found herself becoming nervous suddenly. There was a strange sensation in her stomach that was not unpleasant but was unsettling all the same.

They took their seats at the back of the already full ante-room where the lecture was being held.

"It is better attended than I had imagined," he said to her over the hub-bub of voices. "But it is a small enough room that we have a good view even from the back."

"Yes," she said simply, feeling a little overwhelmed.

Why did it have to change? She had felt at ease as

they talked outside and now, she wondered what she would say next. Holding his arm so lightly could surely not have affected such a change.

"I am looking forward to the lecture." She finally found something to say.

"Indeed. Although, it is not due to start for some ten minutes, I believe." He turned in his seat, looking at her expectantly.

Verity knew that he was keen to continue in conversation and she was dismayed to discover that he did not seem to be suffering from the same blight of romance which she suffered from. Oh, if only she had not spoken to Jane!

"Have you been well since last we spoke?" he asked, embarking on a very ordinary conversation.

"I have... well, yes. Yes, I have been well, thank you," she mumbled and could see him eying her curiously.

"And your brother... is well? Your parents?"

"Yes, they are all well, I thank you," she said and felt her cheeks reddening inexplicably. "And I went to see my sister, Jane."

"And your sister... is well?" he asked slowly and cautiously, studying her in a way that she wished he would not.

"I... well... yes, she is," Verity said and then remembered her manners. "Thank you, Irving."

"Verity, forgive me, but are you suddenly unwell?" He whispered into her ear, not wanting to ask his question aloud in so crowded a room.

But his warm breath on the side of her face just served to make matters worse. She felt ridiculous, so young and unexperienced, and wondered where the dreadful feeling had come from.

"No, I am perfectly well, thank you," she said, realizing that she was not going to enjoy the evening at all.

"Is something else troubling you?" It was clear that he was not going to let it go.

"No," she said and shook her head vehemently. "Well, yes, actually, there is," she said and felt a calmness descend.

Verity realized that her only explanation for her behavior would be the truth. She could not come up with a plausible tale to explain her sudden change in demeanor, for she did not have an ounce of guile anywhere.

"Do tell me, what is it?"

"I feel rather differently towards you than I thought I did. And I am afraid that it has come upon me rather suddenly," she said and took a deep breath. "You see, when I had first suggested to Amos that I write to you and have you accompany me here tonight, he was surprised that I would come without a chaperone of any kind."

"I had wondered the same myself," Irving began. "But then I had assumed that your feelings were such that you were comfortable without one."

"And that is exactly what I had assumed myself," Verity said, finding that the truth was very much setting her free; or setting her tongue free, at any rate. "I have enjoyed our conversations very much and you are a very handsome man, Irving," she said, seeing the suddenly stunned look on his face. "But I did not consider that I had come to think of you as something other than a friend. I did, of course, detect some sympathy between us in the matter of our interests and perhaps even our quietly held opinions of society," she went on. "But when I took your arm this evening, on the way in here, I realized that just because I had not thought about it did not mean it was not there. What I am trying to say is that I have discovered that I like you very much indeed and I have discovered it quite suddenly. Forgive me, for it made me a little tongue-tied and uncomfortable. It is not something that I am used to experiencing, you see, and it took me quite unawares," Verity said and gave him a very simple smile to indicate that she had finished.

"Goodness, you are a very *honest* young woman," he said, now seeming a little tongue-tied himself.

"Forgive me, should I not have been?" Verity asked, feeling all at sea in an area of life she did not know well at all.

"Oh, no, you absolutely should have been," he said and smiled at her, laughing a little as if he could not quite believe it. "I am just taken aback because I have never heard anybody speak so plainly. No wonder you thought the young man creeping along the assembly rooms so amusing. You are very direct."

"I would like to say it is simply because I have always thought it easier to be so, but the truth is that I do not know how to be any different. I am afraid this is my character; this is how I am," she said without any hint of apology.

"And I am glad of it, Verity. I had never dared to hope that I would experience something like this in my life. I am ten years older than you, as you know, and I had quite given up on the idea of finding something like this, something so unusual."

"And you are pleased to find something so unusual?" Verity said, not entirely sure that she understood.

"I am more pleased than I can ever say," he said, and he looked into her eyes for a very long time.

They sat in just such a fashion, quietly looking at one another, until the room fell to a hush and the speaker for the evening cleared his throat and introduced himself.

Without another word, Irving smiled at her and they both faced the front, easier with each other than they had ever been and ready to share the wonder of an interest in common.

CHAPTER TWELVE

or the first time, the dark and somewhat claustrophobic atmosphere of Clarendon's did not bother Irving at all. He had arrived before Amos, but the host recognized him from his previous visits and ordered the clerk to sign him in as a guest.

He was keen to speak to Amos for something had been greatly playing on his mind ever since that wonderful evening in the town hall with Verity.

Her honesty would have knocked him down into his seat had he not already been seated, for he was sure that he had never known a young woman to speak so plainly before. And yet she spoke her truth gently, with poise and dignity, and it had affected him to the very core of his being.

Verity did not go against her mother's undoubtedly careful training in a willful sense, she was just the sort of woman who answered a question truthfully for good or ill. She did not twist things or have another person guess at her mood. She simply declared it there and then and it had been the most refreshing thing that Irving had ever encountered.

Not only refreshing, but it had made him face a little truth of his own. He had known almost immediately that Verity was a young lady he would not only fall in love with easily, but one whom he could love for the rest of his life without ever wondering about another.

And by the time they had parted company and he had taken his own carriage home that evening, Irving knew that he *had* fallen in love with her. He allowed it to surface naturally, without questioning it or trying to rationalize it. He took a leaf from Verity's book and simply looked at the truth and let it be. No denial, no pondering, just plain acceptance.

"The clerk told me that you were already here, my

good fellow," Amos said with a broad smile and his customary hearty tone which, unsurprisingly, drew glances from the more morose in the dining room.

"I hope you are well, Amos?"

"Yes, very. And I would say that you look well too, Irving. This business of happiness is starting to suit you," Amos said with the same teasing smirk he had worn on his face throughout all his years at Eton.

"I believe it is," Irving said honestly.

"Your evening at the town hall went well?"

"It went well. I had not expected it to go so well, especially since Verity did not have a chaperone," Irving said and when he saw Amos' eyes open wide, he rushed to explain. "For heaven's sake, man! What on earth do you think I am about to tell you?"

"Forgive me, I do rather tend to judge other men by my own rather poor standards." His grin resurfaced, and Irving knew that they were back on familiar ground.

"Although I realize you perceive it already, I feel I must tell you that nothing improper occurred at all," Irving said flatly. "But I do believe that your sister and I are moving ever closer to a formal courtship. We spoke a little of it and she admitted very honestly that she feels as I feel."

"I knew it. I knew the two of you would get along if only I could put you together," Amos said triumphantly. "I cannot wait to tell my sister Jane what a fine matchmaker I am. She will be green, my dear fellow. *Green.* She thinks herself such an authority on these things and it turns out that it is I who am Cupid."

"Amos, try to concentrate for a moment, my old friend," Irving said with an expression of exhausted disbelief. "You really are the most excitable man I have ever met."

"Anything to pass the time." Amos turned as if to look for one of the servants. "Where are they all?"

"I am sure somebody will be with us in a moment," Irving said. "As to the subject of you gloating to your sister Jane that you are Hertfordshire's greatest matchmaker, I would beg that you do not."

"But why?"

"In the last days I have begun to grow uneasy with

the manner in which I made your sister's acquaintance."

"What do you mean?" Amos said, looking at him with genuine blankness.

"Well, I did not truly happen upon her in Mrs. Barton's drawing room, did I? In fact, if you had never talked to me of her, I would never have met her at all. But Verity does not know any of this."

"I see." Amos nodded thoughtfully. "Ah, so you would not like her to discover it by my carelessly telling Jane. Yes, I understand perfectly. Have no fear at all, Irving, your secret is safe with me."

"Whilst I am pleased with your uncharacteristic perception, Amos, that is not entirely what I meant. I do not want you to tell it to your sister Jane because I would prefer that Verity hear it from *me*."

"You mean to tell her?" Amos said loudly, causing an elderly gentleman who had seemed to be almost asleep over a steamed pudding to raise his head and tut somewhat forcefully.

"Yes, I think I must."

"But why on earth would you tell the truth?" Amos said, incredulous.

"You are her brother; how can you ask such a question? Why would you not want me to be honest with your own sister? The idea of anything other should make you furious."

"Yes, yes, with any other fellow it would," Amos said earnestly. "But this is a little bit different, is it not? Perhaps the manner of your first meeting was a little contrived, and even the second meeting. Actually, possibly the third as well," Amos said, bungling the whole thing terribly. "But the point is, the rest has been natural, has grown from what is truly there. The little plans are over, and it is time to forget them. It is time for life to be lived. Why on earth would you do or say anything to upset it all now?"

"Then you admit that your sister would not be entirely happy to discover it?"

"It is too hard to tell with Verity. I am sure that you are becoming aware that she is a most unusual young woman. One might say something and assume it would offend only to find her taking the information quite sensibly and rationally. She is not quick to moods or temper, but she is rather a rational sort. She might sit down for a while and wonder if one very small untruth at the beginning of things might indicate a pattern for the rest of her life. She is a thinker, sir. A philosopher and a theorizer, if you will. And I am not enough of either of those things to be able to predict with any certainty that she would take such news without consequence."

"I do not think I like the idea of being anything other than entirely honest with her. You see, Verity has such courage. Her level of honesty requires such courage, you see. And if I do not display the same honesty, I do not display the same courage."

"Then you will get on very well being every bit the philosopher and theorizer that my sister is," Amos said with a modicum of disdain. "Oh, my dear fellow, can you not simply forget it? Let it be?"

"I must admit, I would not like to forfeit her good opinion of me," Irving said slowly, wondering if it really did matter after all.

"That is the spirit, Irving!" Amos said with a broad and boyish smile. "Ah, if you would?" He called loudly across the room, smiling at the approaching servant. "Could I have my usual, please? And the same for my companion if it would suit him."

"Yes, thank you," Irving said, hardly registering Amos' words.

Instead, he was imagining how he would feel to lose Verity. They were hardly courting yet but if she walked away from him now in anger, Irving knew that he would never find anybody to replace her in his heart. He knew that was why he had come to regard her so well and so quickly; there was not another woman in the world like Verity Colchester.

If he spent the rest of his life looking, he knew he would be a very lonely man. And so it was, in that moment, he decided to take the advice of his old school friend. He would say nothing of how it was he had first come to set eyes on her all those weeks ago in Mrs. Barton's drawing room. And if his life took the wonderful turn he had begun to suspect it might, would it really matter in the end?

CHAPTER THIRTEEN

*L*ess than a week later, Verity and Amos made their way to Forton House to have afternoon tea with Irving and his mother.

Verity liked the house very well, for it reminded her somewhat of her father's house. It was of respectable size and wealth, but comfortable rather than ostentatious. The drawing room was decorated warmly, with dark wood furniture, light brocade upholstery, and heavy green velvet curtains. And yet it did not detract from the summer at all, for large windows let in such wonderful light.

"It is such a warm day, Verity," Mrs. Ayres began. "I wonder if you think we should take tea on the terrace instead of in this room?"

They had arrived only five minutes before, and yet Verity was already at her ease with Irving's mother. She was a gentle woman who gave herself time to think before responding to any question; a quality which Verity liked very well for the simple fact that she shared it.

"Oh yes, what a nice idea. It really is so warm, and it would be a shame to miss the day," Verity replied enthusiastically.

"I shall make my way down to let the maids know," Irving said and bowed before disappearing.

"Let us go out through the morning room," Mrs. Ayres said, and Verity and Amos followed her.

The terrace was streaked with warm sunshine, so lovely and bright that Verity had to squint. There was a well laid out seating area, with wrought iron benches and chairs, and a table large enough to accommodate a tea tray when it arrived.

"All done," Irving said when he stepped out through the French windows of the morning room to join them. "Tea will be with us shortly."

"Thank you, Irving," Mrs. Ayres said. "Verity, my

son tells me you are greatly interested in botany," she smiled at Verity and it was clear that her interest was genuine.

"Yes, I have a great interest. I first met Irving when we both went to listen to Mr. Winstanley give a talk on the use of microscopes."

"Irving told me that you have a microscope of your own." Mrs. Ayres looked more interested than ever. "What a thrilling thing. You must have found so much of interest to look at."

"I have." Verity spoke with enthusiasm. "All manner of things, Mrs. Ayres. I have looked at leaves of all kinds, even tree bark. And just last week I cut up a strawberry and put a slice of it on a slide and studied it very closely. They look quite different when magnified, especially the skins. The tiny seeds are so distinct when one looks at them through a microscope."

"You have beaten me to it, Verity," Irving said with a laugh. "I had quite forgotten about strawberries."

"Verity would never have forgotten about the strawberries, Irving," Amos laughed. "She is very steady when she has an idea in her head. She is never happy until it is brought to some conclusion."

"Quite so," Irving said and gave her a slow, handsome smile which made her blush a little.

"That is a very good quality to have, Verity," Mrs. Ayres said with some determination. "A quality you ought never to let go of under any circumstances."

Verity nodded her agreement and wondered what life had been like for Mrs. Ayres with a husband of the type that Amos had briefly described to her.

Would she have been allowed to speak so freely when they had guests if her husband had still been alive? And how was it that the father's influence had not seemed to pierce the son's heart? For Verity was sure now that it had not.

Jane had been right; Verity was blessed with intelligence and absolute rationality and, *of course,* she could discern a man's character. If Irving had been anything like his father, he would not be so obviously respectful of his mother.

Verity was beginning to feel as if all the pieces of life

had started to fit together and fit together well. It all gave her a tremendous feeling of excitement.

"This is a very fine garden, Mrs. Ayres. So many trees and such a lot of interest to it," Verity said, peering out across a smooth sunlit lawn to the trees beyond.

"Thank you, Verity. The gardener deserves all the credit if I am honest."

"Just to the left of the trees there, Verity, you will see that I have some raised beds," Irving said. "I have been growing all manner of plants and herbs for study. There are many which have medicinal properties as I am sure you already know."

"I have read a little on the subject but have really only studied classical botany and have very little idea of the uses of plants for health."

"Perhaps Irving could show you after tea," Mrs. Ayres said and smiled as two maids approached carrying trays.

Verity enjoyed the serenity of the garden and the warmth of the conversation. Mrs. Ayres seemed to like Amos very much, laughing at his amusing comments and prompting him to make more. She really was a very nice woman and Verity thought that she would easily get on with her.

"Would you like to take a little walk across the garden to the herb beds?" Irving asked and smiled at her when tea was finally done.

He looked so handsome wearing dark cream breeches, brown boots, and a brown tailcoat and waistcoat. His blonde hair seemed to glint a little here and there in the sunshine and his skin looked a little more tanned.

"Yes, please," Verity said, looking at Amos and Mrs. Ayres.

"Do go on, my dears," Mrs. Ayres said warmly. "I have Amos to entertain me."

"I shall do my best," Amos said and embarked upon some little piece of gossip he had picked up at the assembly rooms, much to Mrs. Ayres' delight.

Verity and Irving walked across the lawn side-by-side, some little distance apart. It was as if they were both self-conscious about their burgeoning relationship in the company of others. But it was still exciting to her, even though she did not enjoy the luxury of walking arm in arm with him.

"I began with feverfew, Verity," he said the moment they reached the first of the raised flower beds. "I had suffered greatly from headaches, you see, and had read that feverfew was the very thing for such a malady," he said and pointed out the plant to her.

"And did it work?" Verity asked, leaning over the bed just a little so that she might inspect the plant closer still.

"I would not be without this wondrous little plant, Verity. I suppose that was where my interest in the subject began. I had only grown this, you see, as a means of discovering if it really did help to cure headaches. When I realized that it did, when I had the very proof of it, my interest was fully drawn. I wanted to find out what else there was to be discovered."

"And this is St. John's wort, is it not? I have seen it growing wild."

"Yes, it is very good for a low mood. I grew that for my mother when my father was still alive," he said and winced at the unwitting revelation.

"And did it work for your mother?" Verity said without any hint of embarrassment.

"Yes, it worked very well. Although I am bound to say that she has no need of it anymore." Irving gave an irreverent chuckle and Verity could not help but laugh.

"I think that you do not miss your father greatly," Verity said innocently.

"I do not miss him at all." He shook his head. "My mother missed him at first, or at least I believe she *thought* she did."

"Only *thought* she did?"

"It was just such a great change that she struggled to get used to, that is all. She was free suddenly, but she did not realize it. That is the power that some people have over others, I suppose. His control of her seems to extend beyond the grave and I wondered if she would ever become her own person again."

"I do not know her, of course, but it strikes me that she has recovered herself," Verity said tentatively.

"Yes, she has done very well. It has taken these last two years, but she is finally free of that man."

"He was unkind?"

"He was *afraid*, and it made him unkind."

"But what did your father have to be afraid of? Surely not your mother?"

"He was afraid of my mother entirely, but not in the common way. He knew, you see, that my mother was a clever woman. I have no doubt that it was one of the things which drew him to her in the first place. But as with many of his type, the thing he loved her for was the thing he hated her for."

"I do not understand."

"He admired my mother in the beginning. But when he realized that she far outshone him, his insecurities got the better of him and he slowly stripped away everything that was once her. It really was the cruelest thing imaginable, as cruel as if he had been a brute who struck her."

"You would not behave in such a way, I think," Verity said, and whilst she was certain of it, she still wanted to hear it from him.

"I cannot understand why a man would want to live with an empty shell. What better thing in the world than to spend your life with a person who shares your interests and your passions? What a very satisfying thing that would be," he said and was staring directly into her eyes, not letting her go.

"Yes, that would be a very satisfying thing," Verity said, her heart beginning to beat a little faster.

"I hope to be able to prove that you can trust me, Verity. I am myself always and do not change."

"I think I had begun to perceive as much myself, Irving."

"Miss Colchester," he said and took her arm to lead her a little further along to another herb bed. "If you like."

"And you must call me Verity," she said, feeling her heart opening further still.

It hardly seemed possible that so much had changed for Verity in so short a space of time. She had never believed that she would feel so strongly about any man and yet she did. But it had not changed her, not in essentials. Verity had not become another person altogether simply because she found herself falling in love. She was still herself.

And yet she could not deny that the opening of her heart had been a most wonderful thing, for it had allowed her to see that there was truly room for love not only to exist, but to be enjoyed.

"I have come to regard you very highly, Verity." He looked at her with such intensity that Verity could not take her eyes from his face.

She looked at him in wonder and tried to imagine his feelings. Were they the same as her own? Did his stomach feel light and heavy all at once? Did his heart beat a little faster? Did his skin feel hot to the touch?

"I did not know these feelings were possible," Verity was whispering, despite the fact that they were barely in view of her brother anymore. "It has an effect that is physical, Irving. At first, I did not like it," she said, and Irving laughed.

"You are always so honest."

"My mother says that I am blunt."

"You *are* blunt at times, but pleasingly so. Perhaps we think of such things as blunt simply because they are honest. Our world is not used to open honesty."

"Do you like it?"

"Yes. I find I cannot stop thinking about you. My every waking thought, you are there." His voice became heavy and slow. "My every dream."

"I wonder what it is like to be kissed," Verity said, and he straightened up, his eyes wide and his eyebrows raised.

"I would like to kiss you," he said, when he regained the power of speech.

"I like your honesty too," Verity said with a teasing smile.

She waited to be kissed but it seemed that Irving was unsure. He peered over her shoulder before taking her hand and leading her to stand behind a tall raised planting bed filled with willow herb, its thin green leaves and delicate pink flowers spreading wide.

"Did you mean it?" he said, and she could hear his breathing coming fast and a little ragged.

"Yes." Verity looked into his eyes, willing him to see right into her soul.

He gave one final look over her shoulder to be sure

they were not overlooked before taking her gently into his arms. He was so tall that Verity, the smallest of the Colchester women, had to tilt her head back to look up at him. The sun was in her eyes a little, but she narrowed them, making his handsome face come into view wonderfully.

When he pressed his lips against hers, he was so gentle. His lips were so smooth, and Verity so overwhelmed by the feeling that she could hardly catch her breath. And then it was over.

He released her from his embrace, but held on to her hand, gently stroking her smooth skin with his thumb in a most caring, warm gesture.

"That was wonderful," Verity said, her heart cantering and her excitement riding high. "I have never felt such a thing."

"You are so beautiful," he said and looked as if he were dazed by it all.

And in truth, Verity was also. She could hardly believe the events of the last few moments and the wonder of it all was something she would never forget. Perhaps this was why Jane loved the idea of romance so well. Verity had to admit, it certainly felt very good.

"We should return to your mother," Verity said, wishing that they could simply stay right where they were for the rest of the afternoon, embracing and kissing so gently.

"I suppose we must," he said and pulled a face, making Verity laugh. "I hope I am still able to talk sensibly when we get there." He smiled and raised her hand to his lips, kissing the back of it before releasing her completely.

CHAPTER FOURTEEN

"What a very fine day this is, Verity," Jane said as she and Verity wandered about their father's grounds with their brother.

"Yes, the summer is proving to be very warm this year," Verity said in agreement.

"Oh, Verity, I was not talking about the weather," Jane said with a sigh and Amos laughed.

"What?" Verity said, feeling that little confusion she often felt when the three of them were together.

"Even *I* understood that Jane was not talking about the sunshine, sister. She is talking about your wonderful new life. This is the first she is hearing of it and that is what makes it a very fine day, Verity." Amos was still chuckling.

"What a funny world it is when my brother understands such things and my sister does not." Jane was equally amused.

"Well, I am my own character, Jane. I might not always see things as you do, but I am not so sure I would want to. I like to see things the way I see them. In the end, that is what makes me, well, *me*," Verity said a little plaintively.

"I would never want to change you, Verity. I would not change a single thing about you, you are quite adorable," Jane said and linked her arm through her sister's.

"Yes, like an adorable little horse with blinkers on who can only see a straight path ahead and nothing to either side." Amos was in the mood to tease.

"Oh, do be quiet, Amos," Verity chastised him. "You are always teasing me."

"Forgive me, Verity, I thought you liked it. I thought that was what made me such a charming brother to you." He pulled a face, opening his eyes wide and innocently.

"Yes, all right, it *is* what I like about you," Verity admitted. "But you both seem to understand all the things I do not, and I suppose it has become a little worrying to me of late."

"It does not matter how you see things, Verity. And it has never worried you before." Jane stopped walking when they reached the shade of one of the willow trees. "Is something the matter?"

"No, nothing is the matter," Verity objected.

"Perhaps it is because things are changing for you, perhaps you are changing just a little. I daresay it is very disconcerting at times," Jane carried on gently.

"Yes, especially for one who has always..." Amos began but Jane cut in.

"Amos, you are not helping," she said in a low determined voice and Amos smiled and held out his hands in front of him in surrender.

"I suppose things *are* changing. Not everything, I am still the same in essentials. I suppose things have been added to, that there is more to think about than I had ever considered," Verity said truthfully.

"It is not always an easy thing to be in love," Jane said with pride in her own knowledge of the matter. "But it is always wonderful."

"Yes, it is rather wonderful," Verity said, and Jane's eyes immediately shone with tears.

"Oh, Verity, I really could not be happier." Jane threw her arms around her sister and squeezed her tightly. "I wish I could meet this young man of yours. Do say I can meet him soon."

"Yes, you can meet him soon," Verity said and embraced Jane with equal ferocity.

"Oh, you would like him very much." Amos chattered on in the background. "He is a very fine fellow. But he is a clever sort, one who has his little interests and obsessions. He was just the same at Eton," he chuckled. "That is why I thought he would be such a good match for Verity. They are almost exactly the same in certain......"

"I beg your pardon?" This time it was Verity who cut him off.

"I just mean to say that you are well suited," Amos said appearing suddenly flustered.

"No, you said that our similarities were why you thought he would be a good match for me," Verity said in a quietly accusing voice. "And I think I would like you to explain just exactly what you mean by that."

"Verity, it is nothing," Amos said in a tone she recognized well.

It was the tone he had used for years on his parents whenever there was some trouble coming. Whenever he had been caught out in some piece of mischief or other, Amos had always smiled and made very light of it. And Verity was certain that there was some piece of mischief at the root of everything she had thought to be real.

"Amos?" Jane said, releasing Verity but still holding onto her hand. "What is this?"

"It really is nothing. At least it ought not to matter, at any rate," Amos said defensively.

"What ought not to matter?" Jane asked with an air of maternal chastisement.

"That I did not meet Irving by accident," Verity said, feeling the truth of it all hit her with a horrible clarity.

"Does it matter what circumstances you met him in?" Amos said, looking annoyed with himself for having spoken out of turn.

"What circumstances?" Jane went on, clearly not seeing any of it.

"That is why I have never seen him before at Mrs. Barton's house."

"He *is* acquainted with Mrs. Barton and he *did* spend a good deal of time there before his father passed away and his mother needed him," Amos countered. "That is the truth, Verity."

"But he would not have been there that day but... to meet me, would he?"

"Well, well..." Amos faltered.

"No, he would not," Verity finished his sentence for him. "Oh, I see it now." She shook her head, feeling angry and foolish in equal measure. "First it was Mrs. Barton's house and then the woodland. He was not there by accident, he does not walk there."

"As a matter of fact, he *does*," Amos said with certainty.

"And yet you know exactly what I am talking about. If you had no part in it, how would you know that I had ever happened upon Irving in the woodland?"

"I am not trying to hide the truth from you, Verity. I am just trying to tell you that it does not matter."

"And when did the truth cease to matter, Amos?" Verity felt like crying and holding it back could only be achieved by replacing her deep upset with anger. "You told him I would be there. Oh, and then the assembly rooms. I told him I did not like the dancing at the assembly rooms and then you insisted that I go with you. What a fool I have been not to see it!"

"All right, I admit it, I had truly thought that the two of you would get on well. And you have. I know I interfered, but I have not done so for a long time."

"Amos, that does not make it all right," Jane said quietly.

"Why not?" Amos said, becoming a little angry himself. "It is only because I care about you, Verity."

"That is not *caring*, Amos. You interfered because

you did not think I was good enough as I am. You thought that I ought to be married just as my sisters are. Just as everybody else seems to be. You could not simply accept me the way I am. No, there is nothing caring in that."

"Verity, you make it sound quite dreadful and I can assure you that it was anything but." Amos took a step towards her but Verity, so tiny and slight, held one hand up in front of her that managed to stay him as effectively as colliding with a rock might have done.

"It *was* quite dreadful, Amos. Dreadful and cruel. You have led me along a path blindly and I have been foolish enough to open my heart and accept Irving inside it. You have made a fool of me and I shall never forgive you for that."

"But, Verity, Irving does not think you are a fool." Amos looked crestfallen now, his anger all drained away.

"Just leave me alone. From this point onward, Amos, you are not to interfere in my life in any way. For it is *my life*, do you hear me? My life, not your life. And if I choose not to marry ever, then that is my decision, not yours. I will not have you mold me so that I am acceptable to you. If you do not like the way I am, you need not look." And with that, Verity turned on her heel and ran for the house.

She could hear her brother and sister in pursuit, but she was smaller and faster, and she did not stop running until she had dashed to the house, up the stairs, and into her own chamber.

CHAPTER FIFTEEN

*V*erity avoided her brother for two days together, eating her meals in her room and only going down into the drawing room when she was certain he had gone out of the house.

She was sure that it could not be long before Amos sought to interfere again, if he had not done so already. Perhaps he had already told Irving that he had unwittingly given them both away for tricking her so badly.

"There you are, my dear," her mother said gently when Verity crept into the drawing room.

"I had thought you were out, Mama," Verity said and continued into the room, certain that she could not comfortably escape her mother's company now she had been seen.

"I could not go out and undertake charitable works for others as a priority over caring for my daughter, could I?"

"Well, that is very kind, Mama, but you need not have worried. I am perfectly all right." Verity sat down on an armchair.

"Why do you not come and sit by my side, child?" Her mother patted the seat next to her on the couch.

"I would rather sit by myself," Verity said and truly meant it.

"You have always been a little apart from the rest of us. But we all love you dearly, I hope you know that."

"I am not apart, Mama, I am just different."

"Yes, that is a better way of putting it." Her mother did not argue, and Verity was grateful for that. "But I do wish that you would accept a little help now and again."

"I honestly do not need any help, Mama. But I am grateful for your offer," Verity said simply.

"Amos really is very sorry, truly sorry."

"It does not matter how sorry he is for I am not yet ready to forgive him. I do not know if I ever can forgive him for this."

"For caring?"

"For interfering. He has made such a fool of me, and so has Irving. Why would they do such a thing? I know I am unusual, but am I really so amusing that people must poke fun at me all the while?"

"I truly do not think that they had ever intended to poke fun at you."

"And yet that is what they have done."

"I wish you were not quite so angry."

"Really?" Verity said incredulously. "And why is that? Do you not think I have a right to it?"

"I just think that any other young woman might have been pleased for her brother's interest in her life. And then for Mr. Ayres' interest; you have seemed to get along so well."

"Yes, but it was based on a pretense. And you wonder why I am a little apart, as you put it? I have managed to keep myself out of all this silliness in womanhood. I was happy to be myself, to follow my own heart and my own interests. And then I allowed myself to be dragged into it all and I am not only a part of all this silliness now, but I am also at its very core. But I will *never* be made such a fool of again."

"But you like Mr. Ayres, my dear. In fact, I believe that you are very much in love with him. Are you not pleased to be so?" Mrs. Colchester, ordinarily amusing and at ease with her daughters, was now being so very cautious.

"I do like Irving," Verity said, feeling the very words catch in her throat. "But that is not the way I ever wanted my life to be. I am not the sort of woman who would be happy to win her prize, her perfect suitor, without her feelings being absolutely and equally returned."

"I know you would not, and that is not what I am suggesting."

"Then what are you suggesting? And please, be plain in what you say, Mama. I find it hard enough to hold onto the threads of conversation with you, Jane, and Esme at the best of times. But I am currently very out of sorts and I would much rather you say whatever you have to say outright. I am likely not to grasp any hints you might lay down."

"All right, then I shall be plain. You are in love with Irving and I believe that he is in love with you also."

"You do not know him, Mama. And even if you did, why would you believe that? When he has taken part in a game with my brother, the kind and caring brother for whom I am not good enough on my own, why would you think he had any regard for me whatsoever?"

"Because he has come to know you, my dear. Amos assures me that his own interference ceased some time ago and that you and Irving have been making such wonderful progress on your own."

"Irving has lied to me, Mama," Verity said solemnly. "But I was so caught up in it all. Jane told me that I was clever enough to work out any man's character, so much so that I could be sure that such a man would not change when we were married. But she was wrong, was she not? And now I cannot be sure of anything. I cannot think."

"In which case I think you should give yourself a

little time before deciding to be an enemy of your brother and turning your back on Irving. Give yourself time to think, Verity."

"I cannot do it here, I am too distracted," Verity said. "You must let me go to Aunt Mary in Lancaster. Please, I do not want to be here at the moment."

"Oh, but your Aunt Mary is so determined." Elizabeth let out a great sigh. "She is my sister and I love her dearly, but she has become so bossy and opinionated of late."

"Yes, ever since that horrible husband of hers died. I am pleased for her if you are not."

"Verity, that is no way to speak."

"Why not? I mean it," Verity said defiantly. "I like Aunt Mary. I am never left wondering exactly what it is she means for she always says exactly what she means, and she always means exactly what she says. And she will not talk to me of romance and roses for her own marriage taught her that there is more to life."

"That is what I am afraid of. When you are already

in this mood, I cannot help but think that your Aunt Mary will exacerbate it."

"Please, Mama, I do not want to be here at the moment," Verity said truthfully. "Please ask Papa if I can go to Lancaster as soon as possible."

"All right, my dear. As you wish." Mrs. Colchester, realizing that she would get no further with Verity on the subject, rose from her seat and crossed the room.

She paused at Verity's chair and leaned over to tenderly kiss the top of her head.

"Thank you," Verity said, hardly knowing if she was grateful for her mother's gentle care or for the idea that she would be allowed to go to Lancaster after all.

CHAPTER SIXTEEN

*V*erity awoke on her second morning in Lancaster to a beautifully bright summer's day. But the north-west wind was so much stronger than the south-east and she could hear it rumbling in off the Irish Sea.

Verity wrapped her shawl about her shoulders and crossed the neat and pretty chamber that her Aunt Mary had made ready for her when she first arrived. She pulled the curtain back and peered out of the window, the high elevation of the house in Lancaster affording her a wonderful view of the hills to the north in Cumbria, and the Bay of Morecambe and the sea to the west.

With the sun so bright, the sea, just five miles away,

was the deepest and most appealing blue. And yet Verity knew from childhood experiences of sea bathing that the water there was colder than she could stand, despite the fact it looked so inviting.

She had felt instantly relieved to arrive in Lancaster, even after something of an arduous journey on four separate post-chaise carriages. Her mother had already sent a letter ahead of her to let her Aunt Mary know that her youngest niece would soon be arriving. Verity strongly suspected that her mother had given the brief circumstances to Aunt Mary, for she did not seem at all surprised when Verity had first explained it all to her.

But unlike everybody else around her, that fine woman had not sought to excuse Amos' behavior, nor that of Irving's. As far as Aunt Mary was concerned, it had been for Amos *not* to interfere in the first place, and for Irving to be *honest* from the very beginning.

The two men each had a part to play and Verity felt somewhat vindicated to hear that sentiment from her aunt instead of having it dismantled and re-dressed into something much more palatable.

When she washed and dressed and made her way downstairs, her aunt was already sitting in the dining room as the housemaid set out covered dishes of hot food.

Whilst Verity's appetite had not returned altogether, the bacon and freshly baked bread certainly smelled very appealing.

"Good morning, my dear," her aunt said, her face so similar to her mother's and yet her disposition starkly different.

But Verity did not begrudge Mary's voice and the independence she had found in the five years since her husband passed away. The man had been what Verity had always thought of as a very typical kind. In many ways, much the same sort of man as Irving had claimed his father to be. A man afraid to let his wife speak in case it transpired that she knew more than he did.

But her Aunt Mary had not struggled to come to terms with her freedom quite as much when it had finally arrived; she took to it like a duck to water, and took to it rather quickly.

Everyone around her noted the change, with only

Verity's mother recognizing the old spark as something akin to that which Mary had enjoyed in her youth. But even so, Verity's mother had been a little dismayed by her aging sister's sudden return to forthrightness and opinion.

But Verity could understand it entirely. She had managed to put herself in her aunt's shoes and imagine spending the larger part of her life with one hand over her mouth lest she say something intelligent. And Verity could easily imagine what a dreadful strain that would be on a person, how awful such injustice must feel.

And so, Verity did not feel anything but the deepest pleasure for her aunt when her life and her character had become her own again. And of all people, she knew that her Aunt Mary would only ever tell her the absolute truth, whether she wanted to hear it or not.

As far as Verity was concerned, forthrightness in a woman might not be what society desired, but it was something that she knew she could rely on absolutely. That was what mattered to Verity.

"Good morning, Aunt Mary. Goodness, that does smell wonderful."

"Then sit down and start eating, my dear. You are only little as it is, and you are much thinner than you were the last time I saw you. You need a little flesh on those bones of yours."

"Yes, my appetite has been somewhat disordered in the last days. But I suspect that this wonderful breakfast is going to change that," Verity smiled before peering into the dishes. "Oh, warm ham and tomatoes," she enthused before helping herself to a large plateful.

"The first post of the day has been delivered, Verity, and it seems you have a letter." Mary smiled as she handed it across the table to her. "Only your second day and already you have received more letters than I do," she chuckled.

"Oh, it is from Amos." Verity sighed, immediately recognizing her brother's careless handwriting.

"No doubt he seeks to apologize," Mary said in a pleasingly neutral tone.

"I daresay," Verity said, putting down her fork and

hurriedly opening the letter. "Do you mind if I read it at the table?"

"No, as long as you read it out loud," Mary said with a mischievous look.

"Of course," Verity laughed genuinely for the first time in days.

Her Aunt Mary really was making her feel better already, her thoughts were already more ordered.

"He writes," Verity began and cleared her throat.

"My Dearest Sister,

You have only been gone a few days and already I miss you. I suppose it is because I have missed you ever since that day in the garden when I so foolishly spoke out of turn. But I have come to see now that I should have given you the truth in the beginning.

I should have known you better than to interfere in your life, but still I cannot be entirely sorry for doing so. I really do want to see you happy, my dear, even though I now wholeheartedly agree that it was not my business to set things out the way I did.

And yet you did get on so well with Irving Ayres and

he is such a fine man that I found it very easy to trust him with your heart. Even then, I was not sure that you would give it. When you did, I could not have been more pleased.

And I know that Irving was pleased also. More pleased than you no doubt believe, Verity. But I have known how well he regards you even before you and I became sudden enemies in the garden of our home. He had already told me how much he thinks of you, and some weeks ago he mentioned to me his own disquiet at the little subterfuge we had embarked upon in the beginning.

He was most uncomfortable with it and had thought to tell you the truth, obviously explaining that he still likes you very well and for yourself.

But I am afraid that it was I, once again, who made a grave error in this instance and I suggested to him that he say nothing of it. It was my belief at the time that it would make no difference. I could see that his feelings for you had grown greatly and, as the loving brother I do not believe you think I am anymore, I was content that this man would take great care of my sister's heart. And in that spirit, I decided that it was best to forget all about the beginnings and concentrate on all the wonderful things to follow.

And so, you may blame me, my dear, for preventing Irving from being as honest with you as he had wanted to be.

I have spoken to Irving in the days since you went away. I would like to assure you that this was not with a motive to interfere, but rather to explain your absence to him. As you said to me on that day in the garden, the truth does matter. I hope you will not be angry that I have taken your example and chosen to give my old friend the absolute truth.

It is not for me to say, but I shall say it anyway. Irving was greatly disturbed by your sudden departure and even more so to realize that you will unlikely forgive either one of us for all of this. I know that he had visions of a life for the two of you and I am bound to say that I saw in his face the devastation wrought by the idea that those visions might never come to pass.

I do not wish to anger you further, sister, but I would beg you to consider what I have said and search your heart, for I am sure that you will find deep down *inside it a certain knowledge that Irving cares for you deeply, no matter how it was you first met.*

Anyway, I suppose I have gone on for too long and have already interfered more than once in this letter alone. And so, I shall finish here by begging you to forgive me and hoping that you will return to me soon as my loving sister and dearest little friend.

With all my love and in hopes of seeing you very soon,

Your brother,

Amos."

"Well, that was a very pretty letter," Mary said with a smile. "And I am sure that he truly does long for your forgiveness, my dear."

"Yes, I think he does. But I am afraid I am still too angry to give it. I could write to him now and tell him that I forgive him, but what is the point of that when I do not mean it?"

"There is no point in it, Verity, and I would not suggest you do it simply to please Amos and ease his troubles. After all, he is almost thirty-years-old and he is the one who has brought such troubles to himself. He will not expire simply because he does not have your forgiveness when he is ready for it. It is for the forgiver to be ready, not the one who seeks forgiveness."

"That is very true," Verity said and was grateful that her aunt had not allowed her obvious care for her nephew to override her niece's wishes. "And I am glad that he has spoken to Irving, I would not have wanted him to be at a loss as to my sudden disappearance."

"No, I think that little piece of interference was probably necessary. If not necessary, then at least practical." Mary picked up her knife and fork and began to cut into the ham on her plate.

"I wonder if it is true what my brother says, that Irving really did come to care for me in his own right," Verity said, knowing that the opinion of her aunt would be something that could be relied upon.

"I understand that you might find it very difficult to believe such a thing, especially when you have already been somewhat deceived in the origins of your friendship. It is for you to decide in the end, my dear. But I am bound to say that it would be better to hear from the man himself, rather than have your brother be his emissary."

"I could not have put that better myself, Aunt Mary," Verity said and felt settled again.

Something about being away from all of it and in the company of such a sensible woman gave Verity a sense of the rational, an old and familiar sense which was very comforting to her.

"Eat up, my girl. Do not let that newfound sense of appetite fail you now," Mary said and lightly tapped her own plate with her knife to make a point.

"Thank you, Aunt Mary," Verity smiled before tucking into her breakfast.

CHAPTER SEVENTEEN

*W*ithin a few days, Verity had already developed something of a comforting routine. Not far from her aunt's stone-built house was a very pretty little piece of land called Fenham Carr, with trees and pathways and a good deal of peace and quiet.

Verity had been taking morning walks there daily, enjoying the solitude and developing something of an interest in the local birdlife. She was not entirely sure, but she had an idea that there was a greater variety there in Lancashire than there was in Hertfordshire. But perhaps it was simply because she was looking more closely.

In any case, Verity was certain that she had seen a

small yellowhammer on her first day and had spent the next few days sitting quietly and staring up into the trees for any sign of it again. It had been such a fleeting glance, and yet she had been certain. And finding a small illustrated book of British birds in her aunt's small library, she had been quite certain that her identification had been correct.

"Have you lost something?" Came a voice behind her as she sat on a large rock peering upwards into the trees.

The voice pierced the silence and startled her so badly that she turned sharply and almost fell off the rock. Her mouth fell open when she saw none other than Irving himself standing there.

"What are you doing here?" she said, not enquiring after his well-being in the accepted way.

But the accepted way of things was not Verity's way of things.

"I am enjoying a walk," he said, answering in her own literal style.

"Then I will not detain you, Sir," Verity said sharply.

"And yet I would be very pleased to be detained by

you, Verity," he said, annoying her by using her Christian name.

She had only given him authority to do it on that wonderful, terrible day. The day when she had truly opened her heart to him and had welcomed that beautiful kiss. She closed her eyes for a moment, willing herself not to think about any of it. It had been the one thing which had truly hurt her right down to her very bones.

And it had been the one thing that she could not explain to anybody. She could not tell any member of her family that she had willingly kissed him that day and had found it to be the most wonderful experience of her life. She could not explain adequately from the very depth of her heart how truly betrayed she had felt to discover the truth in the end. He had lied to her, and then he had kissed her. It was the closest to having her heart broken that Verity had ever been and it was not an experience that she would willingly walk into again.

"Why are you in Lancaster, Mr. *Ayres*?" she said, pointedly addressing him in a rather more formal manner.

"I am taking a little holiday, *Verity*," he said, using her Christian name with equal pointedness. "I am staying at a coaching inn at Hest Bank."

"And you expect me to believe that *that* is your only reason for being here?"

"No, I have come here in hopes of seeing you," he said and stared at her intently. "That is my primary reason for coming all this way."

"Ah, so you will not lie to me again?"

"No, I will not," he said and looked suddenly downcast. "But if you will not hear me out, I will simply continue with my excursion here as a holiday."

"Then I hope you enjoy yourself."

"I will likely not enjoy myself, but I will find some way to spend my time," he said, and she could see that he had perceived that he had wasted his efforts.

"Very well," she said simply.

"I intend to visit the stone graves at Heysham," he said, changing the subject entirely.

"What?" Verity said, squinting at him.

"I am surprised you have not been already," he said, his tone becoming that which she recognized from their early meetings, the times when they had talked of all the things which had interested them. "There is the ruin of a chapel in Heysham Village just south of Morecambe," he began.

"Yes, I am aware of Heysham Village."

"On the headland overlooking the sea in that area is the ancient ruin of St. Patrick's Chapel. And there is a line of stone graves which are thought to date back to the eleventh century. They have apparently been hewn from the solid rock and I am very keen to see them."

"My aunt has never told me about them, but such things are not particularly of interest to her," Verity said, beginning to feel as if she had missed out on something.

"I intend to visit the area this week. You are more than welcome to join me if you would care to share a carriage. I am certain that it would be of interest to you if nothing else," he said and looked into her eyes just as he had done on that day in the grounds of his home.

Once again, she thought of how he had taken her into his arms and kissed her and she gritted her teeth hard and closed her eyes to dispel it.

"No, I will visit the graves some other time," she said sharply.

"Well, it seems I have outstayed my welcome." He took in a deep breath, straightened up, and seemed to relax in a somewhat resigned way. "I shall bid you a good day, Verity. I hope you enjoy the rest of your stay and, if you have a mind to, I would welcome a visit to the coaching inn in Hest Bank."

"Enjoy the rest of your stay, Mr. Ayres," she said and turned her head to look back up into the trees in a blind search for the elusive yellowhammer.

CHAPTER EIGHTEEN

"And he appeared in Fenham Carr, you say?" Aunt Mary said with surprise. "Just out of the blue?"

"It will not have been just out of the blue, although that is exactly as it appeared to me. I was rather surprised," Verity said and reached out gratefully for the scalding hot cup of tea. "But he will have been here long enough to discover my routine. He would have studied me, for he is already well versed in such an activity."

"Yes, I daresay he is," Mary said slowly. "So, he has come here to apologize? To explain?"

"If he did, I did not let him do it."

"So, he has returned to Hertfordshire?"

"No, he declares that he will stay for a few days at the coaching inn at Hest Bank and treat his visit to Lancashire as a little holiday."

"And you believe that, do you?"

"Well, he did say that he intended to visit the stone graves at Heysham and the ruins of the chapel." Verity shrugged.

"I cannot think that he really means to do that," Mary said a little cynically.

"Oh yes, he will," Verity said with certainty. "He is greatly interested in such things and I am certain that he will make his way to Heysham for the day."

"Are you sure?" Mary was still doubtful that anybody could enjoy a day spent in such a fashion.

"He really does have such an interest in things of that nature. I could see it in his eyes, even as he stood there in Fenham Carr. He becomes so engrossed in a subject of interest, you see. It washes over him, and he absorbs every part of it. I suppose that is why I liked him so very well."

"Perhaps because you are so similar yourself, Verity. I daresay that you would enjoy a day spent at Heysham Village looking at the little ruins."

"Yes, I would. But not with Mr. Ayres, I told him I did not want to go with him."

"And so, he asked you, did he?"

"Yes, he did. He said that we might share a carriage if I wanted to go."

"And do you want to go?"

"I think I would like to see the stone graves very much. I had never heard of them before, you see, and Irving said that they are believed to date back to the eleventh century." Verity became a little wide-eyed. "He said that they have been hewn from the very rockface. The graves were not placed there, they were cut there, so to speak."

"And *now* who is allowing their interest to wash over them so that they might fully absorb it?" Mary laughed. "I suppose I ought really to have taken you there at some point over the years. I should have realized that it would have been just the sort of thing to interest you," she laughed.

"I suppose that I do have somewhat unusual tastes," Verity said wistfully.

"And what is the matter with that? You do not have to be the same as everybody else, do you? Your interests are your own, my dear. They are yours for a lifetime if you will hold onto them and not allow another to take them from you as I once did."

"Was my uncle very awful?"

"Yes, he was," Mary began. "He was a very small-minded man and rather a jealous one. I wish I had not married him when I was still so very young. I was but seventeen, my dear, and very foolish indeed."

"But you were clever even then, Aunt Mary, surely. Did you not see him for what he was before you married him?"

"Oh yes, I could see it even then. But I chose *not* to see it, for I was so keen to be married to him. But I had years and years to repent at my leisure, did I not?"

"So, it *is* possible to know a man's character early on? To see the things which will only make themselves worse with time?"

"Oh yes," Mary said solemnly. "I believe that wholeheartedly. I suppose you are wondering if this Mr. Ayres is truly a bad character."

"I am just wondering why it was I did not see it. After all, I am clever enough, am I not?"

"You are very clever, my dear."

"Then why did I not know him for a liar when I first met him? And why did I not pick up on it as I spent more time with him after that?"

"I suppose because telling a lie does not necessarily make one a liar. Not a perpetual liar, at any rate."

"I am afraid I am growing a little confused, Aunt Mary. I begin to wish that I had never allowed myself to wander down this little path; that little path which promises happiness at the end of it. It is most confusing and not at all rational."

"I believe it is not supposed to be rational exactly. But there are rational thoughts to be had around its outskirts; ideas and instincts which ought really to save us from our own worst excesses."

"Like knowing a person's character?"

"Yes, just that."

"But now I have solid information, do I not?"

"You do. But I am bound to say that my opinion of the man has risen just a little today," Mary said cautiously. "I am not telling you how you ought to proceed, my dear, only that I have a grudging admiration for a man who would make such a journey with the intention of apologizing and explaining, even if, as you say, you did not give him the opportunity."

"Do you think I should have?"

"I really cannot say. That is a question for you, Verity, not me. I am simply saying that he chose to come and face you. To stand before you, not to send a letter and take the easy way out. I had assumed him to be a coward, you see, thinking that he was content simply to have his feelings conveyed to you via a third party. Now I see that he had likely already embarked upon his journey here by the time your brother had chosen to write to you."

"Perhaps that is something I ought to give a little thought to," Verity said, feeling all at sea once again.

As shocking as it had been to see him suddenly there so many miles away from where she thought he was, there had been some pleasure in it, just a little, hiding away beneath all her pride and annoyance.

He really was such a handsome man and, she knew, the only man she had ever been particularly close to. She had thought that he had understood her so well, had even been a little like her. Had all of that really been a lie? Or had it been the truth, albeit built on a lie?

"No, this will not do. I feel as confused now as I did when I sat with my mother in the drawing room at home. I have come here to be able to think clearly without the distractions of the people I see every day. And now one of those people has followed me here and once again I am thrown into disarray. No, I shall not be going out to the coaching inn at Hest Bank to see Irving. If I am to get to the bottom of things, I shall need to do it without such distractions."

"Well, perhaps in a day or two you and I could visit the stone graves at Heysham. It might take your mind off things and divert you well enough. It might even help you to see things a little more clearly."

"Very well, yes. I think I would like that, Aunt Mary. But will you not be terribly bored?"

"Oh yes, I will be terribly bored, my dear," Mary said with her customary honesty. "But I should be glad to be bored if only to help my dear little niece."

"Thank you, Aunt Mary," Verity said, and wondered if there might be any books in her aunt's library about the history of Heysham Village.

CHAPTER NINETEEN

*J*ust two days later found Verity and her aunt climbing out of the carriage in the picturesque village of Heysham ready to make the short walk to the ruins.

Whilst Verity had not been able to find a book on the history of Heysham in her aunt's library, she had managed to purchase a small pamphlet from a bookseller in Lancaster which gave the history of the old chapel and the stone graves.

And in Verity's normal style, she had studied the pamphlet from one end to the other in readiness for the trip. But she had not enjoyed it as much as she ordinarily did when faced with a new area of interest. Her concentration had been wavering and, more than once, she thought of Irving.

Sitting in the drawing room at her aunt's house as that good woman snored gently by the fire, Verity had almost found herself in tears when she thought of how well she would have enjoyed the subject if she and Irving had been able to discuss it as they had so many other things.

She had always adored her pastimes, but she began to realize that she had enjoyed them all the more for being able to share them with another person who was equal in his passion about such things.

Verity realized that the loss of such a wonderful connection, even one that had only been hers for a short while, had made her feel rather lonely in her quest for knowledge about the stone graves.

"You are very quiet, my dear," her aunt said as they walked arm in arm past a very pretty church called St. Peters.

"I am feeling a little low, Aunt," Verity admitted. "And I am also having to concentrate rather hard. I am not used to walking on cobblestones and they seem to be everywhere here."

"I am so used to it that I am hardly a southerner at all anymore," Mary laughed. "But it really is the shortest walk, see? Through that archway is the beginning of the ruins."

"Oh yes," Verity said, brightening a little as she peered through the archway to the grey stone beyond. "Yes, I see." She quickened her pace over the treacherous cobblestones, suddenly keen for a diversion that would overwhelm her.

She took the steps up to the remaining walls of the chapel carefully, for they were very steep. Her aunt followed her with surprising speed and agility and Verity had only looked back once to be sure that she was managing.

"Here we are," Mary said in an attempt at displaying interest which made Verity laugh. "And over there are the stone graves. But be careful, the hill drops away very sharply there, and I would not like to see you fall over the edge in your haste."

But Verity could not answer; she had fallen silent. There, standing and staring down into the stone graves was a shape she recognized entirely. It was

Irving. He had not seen her, for his attention was drawn.

Verity looked back at her aunt with some dismay and realized that she did not seem at all surprised to see a man standing there at all.

"It is him. It is Irving," Verity said, with an instinct that her aunt already knew it.

"I know, my dear sweet girl. I sent him a note and told him when we would be here," Mary said bluntly, and Verity could hardly believe what she was hearing.

Her mouth fell open and she glared at her aunt with open accusation.

"And yes, I am just one more person interfering in your life, Verity. And believe me, I do not do so lightly, for I would not like it at all myself." Her aunt stood squarely in front of her and took her hands, holding them rather tightly. "I would never have sought to find a man for you ever, not for a moment. I would never tell you who to forgive or not to forgive, and I would never tell you who to spend the rest of your life with. But there is something you should know about interference, for all interference is not the same. That is not to say that interference is not wrong, for I am bound to say that I believe it is."

"Aunt, speak plainly," Verity said and felt suddenly exhausted.

"I should not have interfered, but I did. And I did so for the very same reason that Amos did. It is because I love you so very much, child," she said, speaking very plainly indeed. "The thing about interference is, I discover, that it is perhaps not such a bad thing when it is not *enforced*. Tell me, my dear, have you ever heard the expression that you may lead a horse to water, but you cannot make it drink?"

"Yes, of course I have heard it. It is a well-known expression, is it not?" Verity said waspishly.

"And you understand its meaning?"

"Yes, of course I do." Verity was beginning to lose patience. "It means that you can attempt to influence a person, but it does not mean that they will succumb to your influence."

"Goodness, you really are very succinct," Mary said and smiled broadly. "But anyway, what I am trying to say to you is that it is *your* choice whether or not you follow the path that somebody else's interference has set you upon. Once their interference is done, it is done. From that point onward, everything is your choice."

"And so, whilst you have brought the two of us together, it is still my choice whether or not I approach Irving now?" Verity said, asking herself as much as she was asking her aunt.

"Precisely. You may walk over there and hear him out, or you may take my arm now and we will go back to the carriage and he will never know."

"At least you are honest," Verity said, already forgiving her aunt's interference for the fact that it had been so plainly owned up to. "Thank you, Aunt Mary." Verity leaned forward and kissed her aunt's cheek.

"If you do not mind, I shall make my way back to the carriage. I am afraid that ruins rather remind me of my own increasing age." Mary pulled a face and Verity laughed.

"I shall not be long."

"As you wish," Mary said and already began to descend the steep stairs.

As she approached, Irving was still standing with his back to her at the edge of the stone graves, staring out into the Irish Sea as it lapped about the edges of Morecambe Bay.

"Irving?" she said gently, and he turned around. "Oh, do be careful, my aunt says it is awfully steep there."

"Yes, it is." He turned back to peer doubtfully over the edge. "But I am quite safe." He smiled at her. "I am glad you came."

"Irving, I know you had something you wanted to say to me the other day in Fenham Carr, and I am sorry that I did not listen. But I was so angry, you see, so very upset. I felt so foolish and I have done ever since I discovered the origins of our friendship."

"I made a terrible mistake in not being honest with you from the very first. So, I shall be honest with you now, Verity."

"Very well," she said and took a step closer.

"When your brother first approached me about

seeking your acquaintance, I only agreed to it to keep him quiet. You know how he is, you are his sister after all. He is like a wasp buzzing about your ears and the effect only increases unless you give in." He paused, and Verity laughed, entirely recognizing the description of the brother she knew in her heart she still loved completely. "I had never imagined for a moment that I would find you so interesting. Unusual, yes, but all the more interesting for it."

"Is that a compliment?" Verity asked quite seriously, and he laughed.

"Yes, Verity, it is a compliment."

"Then, thank you."

"When your brother suggested that I seek you out again and told me how well you liked to walk in the woods, I was more pleased than I had imagined. You see, I *do* walk in that woodland often and I liked the idea of a lady who enjoyed similar pastimes to myself. But I was quite convinced on that meeting that I ought to give the whole thing up for I was certain you were not at all interested."

"But you went to the assembly rooms anyway."

"Because your brother was so determined that I not give up.... No, that is not true," he said and shook his head. "Or at least it is only partly true. I would have refused him at that moment but there was something in me that needed to know more. A young woman with her own microscope cutting off great lumps of tree bark with her own knife certainly warrants a little further investigation," he said, and Verity laughed again.

"I suppose there are not many men who would think so."

"I have long since stopped trying to behave as other men, Verity. To be anything other than yourself is a very short road to unhappiness and I believe you understand that better than anybody."

"Yes, I do."

"But that night in the assembly rooms, I had never enjoyed myself so much. We had such an open conversation, so smart and engaging, and that was the moment I began to fall for you. And from then on nothing your brother could do or say would influence me in any way at all. I had more or less forgotten how we began, I was just glad that we had. But I had not forgotten it completely; I knew that I ought to have said something to you and I did not." He blew out a great lungful of air. "And I am sorry for that, Verity. It was the wrong thing to do and I am truly sorry."

"So, you did not continue to share my company out of an obligation to my brother?" she said, knowing that this was the very question which had given her so much uncertainty.

"Can you really believe that, Verity? When I took you into my arms and kissed you, do you really think that I did not mean that with all my heart?"

Verity closed her eyes and remembered that moment afresh.

Only this time she remembered it with all the wonder and excitement that overwhelmed her every time she had thought about it in the days which followed. The pain and the feelings of foolishness had all but evaporated.

"Now, I do not. I believe you, Irving," Verity said, opening her eyes to see that he had moved to stand directly in front of her.

They were but inches apart and she looked up into

his face, just as she had done on that wonderful day in his garden.

"I love you, Verity," he said and placed a hand on either side of her face before gently kissing her.

"I love you too, Irving," she said when he released her. "I was just so afraid that you did not really like me. I felt so foolish."

"And I am sorry that I made you feel that way, for I would never have chosen to. Verity, you are the only woman in the world I could ever be in love with. You are the only one who has ever truly meant anything to me."

"And you would not want to change anything about me? Not my bluntness nor my interests nor my determination to follow them?"

"Nothing. You are perfect, Verity, why would I ever want to change anything about you?"

"Would you like to meet my aunt?" Verity asked, smiling up at him.

"Yes, I would like to meet her very much. I would like to thank her," he said and cast a quick look about him once more before kissing her again.

"I know I got into terrible trouble for all of this, but I have to say it was worth it," Amos said as Irving helped his new wife into the carriage outside the church. "If I were a boastful sort of a man, I would probably be patting myself rather hard on the back," Amos went on and everybody laughed.

"Then thank goodness you are so modest," Verity said, settling her wedding gown about her in the carriage so as not to crease it.

"Oh, Verity, it was such a beautiful service." Jane leaned against the door of the open-top carriage with a tear-stained face full of absolute joy. "And what a wonderful little bride you make. So small and pretty, like a little doll."

"Oh, Jane, do not cry again," Verity said in an amusingly strained tone.

"Let her have her fun," Esme said, standing at Jane's side and smiling brightly. "She has been looking forward to this moment almost as much as she looked forward to her own wedding. Do not deny her the simple pleasure."

"Goodness, Esme, we are all married now, are we not? Every single one of the Colchester girls are now spoken for," Verity said and realized that she could not be happier.

"This is why I took such a lenient approach, you see," Edward said as he and his wife stood at the other side of the carriage. "I knew that my daughters would sort themselves out very nicely," he went on and Mrs. Colchester looked at him askance.

"Is it any wonder that we have a son who would take credit for the sky being blue when the father is thus?" she said and shook her head from side to side. "Really, my husband."

"I will miss you both very much," Verity said, looking at her parents and holding back her unexpected tears. "But I shall not be very far away."

"We know, my sweet," Mrs. Colchester said. "But your life is for living, my dear. It is for making your own and for doing things in your own way. We know that we shall see you again."

"We are a family still, are we not?" Esme said as Jane nodded vigorously, tears streaming down her face. "And we shall always be a family. It is just that there are a few more of us now and I daresay there are more to come in the future."

"Oh dear," Verity said and stared thoughtfully into space. "Do you know, I had not really thought about that." And, as everybody began to laugh, she stared at them sincerely. "What is so funny now?"

"It is just you, my darling. It is your wonderful way of putting things," Irving whispered into her ear. "And having children does not put a stop to your interests. It just gives you more people to share them with, that is all."

"Oh, now that sounds like a fine idea," Verity said

thoughtfully after a moment or two of mulling it over.

"And you are happy? Really happy?" he whispered again, taking her hand in his.

"I could not be happier, Irving. I love you with all my heart and I could never imagine my life without you."

"In that case, shall we go home?"

"Yes, let us go home."

"I will love you forever," he said, before they turned to their family and friends to bid them farewell.

IF YOU ENJOYED this book don't miss the other 2 Colchester Sister's books. Get Esme's book here

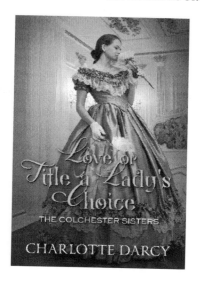

Or Jane's book here

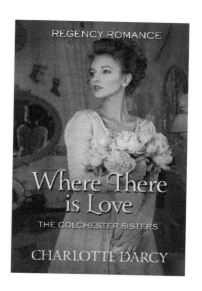

THE BEAST AND THE BARON'S DAUGHTER PREVIEW

"Now then, we really must start packing. I know we shall not be leaving until Friday, but one can never be too well prepared," Lady Ariadne Milford said as she heaved herself to her feet with her customary noisy groan. "Goodness, old age is catching up with me."

"Shall I ask the housekeeper to have your wooden trunk laid out in your room, My Lady?" Jane asked and hoped that she was being helpful. "And then, perhaps, you could tell me what you need, and I could help you pack."

"Not at all, my dear. The housekeeper has everything under control and my lady's maid will pack for me. She is well versed on my traveling needs, Jane." Lady Ariadne gave Jane a reassuring smile. "No, I think you and I shall take tea instead and discuss this nephew of mine. I daresay it will be of some use to you to know a little something of him before we arrive at Sotheby Hall." She looked across the drawing room to the bell rope hanging neatly by the side of the chimney breast. "I know it is early, my dear, but what-say you ring for tea anyway?"

"Of course, Lady Ariadne," Jane said and dutifully rose from her perch on the couch and silently hurried across the room.

"My dear, you are always so keen to help with everything." Lady Ariadne was studying Jane as she made her way back across the room. "But you really are only my companion, Jane. You must try not to be one of my servants, for you are not. I know the circumstances of your father's passing have made you nervous, but you are still a well-bred young woman. None of us know in our youth how the world is going to treat us, but we always have our breeding to fall back upon."

"You are very kind, Lady Ariadne." Jane settled back on the very edge of the couch opposite her mistress.

"Oh, do sit comfortably, Jane. You make me feel as if there is some emergency that I am not yet aware of." Lady Ariadne waved her companion back into her seat. "That's it, lean back a little at least. Is that not more comfortable?"

"Yes, thank you," Jane said and wished she could find some way to feel at her ease.

But her life had been turned upside down with the passing of her father and she felt like a fish out of water.

Her father, Lord Briars, a baron, had struggled for most of his life with a failing estate, doing everything in his power to see it continue for generations to come, even if his heir was to be his nephew. Jane had been his only child and his only relief had been to know that his nephew would have happily kept Jane safe on the estate when the time came. But when the time did come, there was nothing left for Jane's cousin to inherit and no way for that fine young man to add her to his already great responsibilities. In the end, Jane had taken matters into her own hands and struck out into the world in search of a job. Thinking first to try for a position as a governess, she had found luck at last when the very first post she had been offered had been as a companion to Lady Ariadne Milford. It was better paid and kept her status at least a bit better elevated than if she had become a governess.

"Now then, about my nephew," Lady Ariadne began, bringing Jane back into the here and now. "I have not yet told you much about him. The truth is that I did not think he would agree to see me and so I thought there was little point in giving you any of the details before now."

"I see," Jane said, not really seeing but feeling she ought to add to the conversation in some way.

It wouldn't do for her to simply smile benignly and stare out of one of Brockett Hall's ceiling-height windows or to admire the largest fireplace she had ever seen. Lady Ariadne liked her companion to be just that; a companion. She was expected to participate, to give opinions, even offer advice on occasion. But with a woman of such a forceful character as Lady Ariadne, such confidence was not easily found.

"Oh, but he was such a dear boy to me, Jane. Such a handsome little lad." Lady Ariadne looked suddenly upset and Jane, unused to dealing with such things, began to fear she had no means by which to manage. "And when he set off for Spain, his father and me pleading with him to reconsider, he was so full of enthusiasm for life and everything in it." Quite out of the blue, Lady Ariadne dabbed at her eyes with a handkerchief.

"Lady Ariadne, what is it? What is upsetting you?" Jane, feeling certain that her mistress would not want her to dash across the room and comfort her physically, decided to get to the heart of the matter.

After all, it was Lady Ariadne's way of doing things and Jane could only hope that she would appreciate a little forthrightness.

"Oh, I am upset my dear. Very upset. I am always this way when I think of my poor dear Nathaniel."

"Your nephew? But why?"

"He was so terribly wounded out there in Spain. Oh, how I wish he would never have gone."

"Lady Ariadne, forgive me, but is your nephew an invalid on account of his wounds? Is that why you are so upset?" Jane spoke gently.

"No, he is not an invalid, except that he makes himself so." Lady Ariadne, just as her character dictated, sniffed in a loud and unladylike manner without apology, forcing Jane to stifle an inappropriate laugh.

"I do not understand."

"He has made himself a recluse. That handsome boy who left home at just twenty is now a man of thirty who might just as well live in a cave for all the people he sees. He has made himself a hermit."

"And that is why you did not think he would agree to your visit?"

"Yes." Lady Ariadne blew her nose with all the grace of a farmhand. "But he has, and so I must be pleased. And I am, although I suppose it is true to say I am more relieved than anything. I have not seen him for two years. Before that it was three." She shrugged. "I just hope that he will let me help him this time. Let *us* help him," she said and looked meaningfully at Jane.

As Jane smiled kindly, she wondered just what was going to be expected of her.

Find out in The Beast and the Baron's Daughter for just 0.99 and FREE with your Kindle Unlimited subscription.

More Books by Charlotte Darcy

If you love Regency romance join my newsletter for exciting new release announcements and to see my visits to British Regency houses join here. You will receive occasional free content.

A few selected books I hope you will enjoy.

Charlotte

All my books are FREE on Kindle Unlimited

The Lady and the Secret Duke

Love for the Hidden Lady

Love for the Hidden Rose

Box Sets

Regency Romantic Dreams 4 interlinked novels

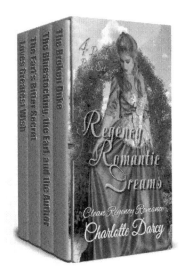

Love at Morley Mills 6 Book Box Set

including an exclusive book in one 6 book collection FREE on Kindle Unlimited.

Love Against the Odds an 11 Book Regency Box Set

More Books by Charlotte Darcy

If you love Regency romance join my newsletter for exciting new release announcements and to see my visits to British Regency houses join here. You will receive occasional free content.

A few selected books I hope you will enjoy.

Charlotte

All my books are FREE on Kindle Unlimited

The Lady and the Secret Duke

Love for the Hidden Lady

Love for the Hidden Rose

Box Sets

Regency Romantic Dreams 4 interlinked novels

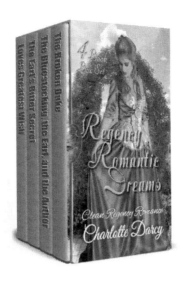

Love at Morley Mills 6 Book Box Set including an exclusive book in one 6 book collection FREE on Kindle Unlimited.

Love Against the Odds an 11 Book Regency Box Set

ABOUT THE AUTHOR

I hope you enjoyed these books by Charlotte Darcy.

Charlotte is a hopeless romantic. She loves historical romance and the Regency era the most. She has been a writer for many years and can think of nothing better than seeing how her characters can find their happy ever after.

She lives in Derbyshire, England and when not writing you will find her walking the British countryside with her dog Poppy or visiting stately homes, such as Chatsworth House which is local to her.

You can contact Charlotte at CharlotteDarcy@cd2.com or via facebook at @CharlotteDarcyAuthor

Or join my exclusive newsletter for a free book and updates on new releases here.

Printed in Great Britain
by Amazon